You Mocha Me Crazy

Tia Marlee

A Novel Choice Press

Book Cover by Beck and Dot

Editing by Lia Huntington

Proofread by Jammom Reads

This book is dedicated to my favorite beta reader, my daughter, Lily. Without her constant encouragement, brutal honesty, and unwavering faith in me, I wouldn't be able to do what I do.

Contents

Chapter One

Aurora

EXCITEMENT PULSES THROUGH ME as I push open the glass door of the Coffee Loft. The aroma of freshly brewed coffee and the hum of conversation always feels like home, but today, there's an anticipation in the air. I look at my watch, relieved to see I'm not *too* late. "Hey, Ashlan. Thanks for opening for me."

"Good morning, Aurora," Ash says, wiping coffee grounds from the countertop. "It's been steady this morning. Lacey's already on her second cup over there." She nods to the corner booth where Lacey's surrounded by colorful brochures and stacks of papers.

As if she heard us talking about her, she looks up and spots me at the counter. "Aurora! You're here, *finally!*" Lacey waves me over, her grin stretching from ear to ear. She waves her hands over the mess on the table. "I've been here for a while."

I shake my head. "Of course I'm here. I told you I'd be here at nine."

Lacey points to the clock above the counter. "It's 9:20."

"Close enough," I say, stepping behind the counter to make myself my favorite White Chocolate Mocha Latte. "Besides, Ashlan was opening. I didn't have to be up at the crack of dawn today." I yawn, covering my mouth with my shirtsleeve.

Lacey laughs. "For someone who owns a coffee shop, you sure aren't a morning person. Come on, Reid will be here soon, and I want to go over these plans again." Lacey's eyes gleam with excitement. "I've been up all night rethinking what I want. Look at these designs. What do you think?"

"I think you should have gotten some sleep," I say, winking at her. I lean in and examine the pencil drawings on the table. "These are amazing, Lacey! I like the addition of the check-in area. That's a great idea to keep the kids from running out of the building without an adult."

"I was thinking of adding some little tables here for the parents who don't want to be in the play area at the front. They can grab a coffee and danish from the Coffee Loft, and then have a seat and enjoy their treat while watching their kids." She sketches a few round tables in the currently empty space. "Is it too much?"

I shake my head. "No, I think it's all great."

She sighs and leans back in the chair. "Do you think I'm crazy? This feels crazy." She reaches for her coffee mug and moves to stand. "I'm getting another coffee."

Laughing, I grab the mug. "I think that's enough coffee for now. You already can't sit still. Seriously, Lacey, this is a great idea and you've got some really great plans here. It's going to be perfect."

Lacey sits back in the booth and lets out a shaky breath. "I don't know why I'm so nervous. I've dreamed about this for years, and partnering with you—joining the spaces—it's better than I could have ever imagined."

"We're doing something special here. I just know it." Piney Brook could use an indoor space for preschoolers to play. The only indoor playground is at the local fast food joint, and it often smells like pee.

Opening a learning space where kids can do art, play dress-up, take music and science classes at an age-appropriate level will be an enormous benefit to the community. Attaching it to the Coffee Loft is just icing on the cake. Parents won't be able to resist grabbing a grown-up treat while their kids are playing. A winning combination . . . or at least, that's what the financial advisor my dad hired to go over the plan said.

"Absolutely," Lacey agrees. "Here's to the Coffee Loft and Matti's Playhouse—the start of something extraordinary."

Just then, the door chimes and in walks a man who's dressed to the nines in an impeccably tailored suit. Its sharp lines emphasizing his broad shoulders. He's handsome in a conventional way, and I wonder why I haven't seen him before. Quickly, I run my fingers across my lips to make sure I'm not actually drooling.

"Reid," Lacey calls, jumping up from her seat and waving. "Over here."

Mr. Tall, Dark and Handsome makes his way over to our table. Figures he would be the guy that Lacey says is in love with her friend Briella.

One of these days, my prince charming will walk into the Coffee Loft and sweep me off my feet. I just know it. Apparently, today is not that day.

"Reid, this is Aurora. She's the owner of the Coffee Loft."

"Majority owner," I interrupt. Dad's an investor, and a partial partner. I was hesitant to agree to involve him at first, preferring to stand on my own two feet, but his business knowledge and experience has turned out to be incredibly helpful.

"Aurora, this is Reid. He's the best architect in the county." Lacey points to the empty booth across from me and gives me a pointed look. "Sit, I'll get you a coffee."

Reid slides into the booth and smiles. "It's nice to meet you, Aurora." He glances at the table and his eyes go wide. "I see you two have been doing some pre-planning."

I laugh. "You could say that. Lacey's been agonizing over what she thinks will be the perfect layout." I wave my hand over the table. "As you can see, she's been busy."

He chuckles. "I see that."

Lacey walks up and sets a coffee mug in front of Reid before sliding into her seat with a glass of water. Thank goodness. If she has any more coffee, I'm afraid she'll be bouncing around the dining room like a jumping bean.

"So," Reid says, after taking a sip of his coffee. "Why don't we walk through the space next door first? Lacey, you can tell me what you're thinking as far as layout. We can decide where the best place to create the connection for the two spaces will be, and we can go from there."

Lacey grins. "Sounds good!" She slips out of the booth and gathers up the papers and brochures she's laid out, tucking them under her arm.

"While you two do that, I'll be in my office doing payroll." I slide out of the booth and wait for them to move toward the front door.

"Oh, no! You need to come," Lacey says. "We need to figure out the best spot to put the doorway. You heard the man." She pauses and sticks out her bottom lip. "Please?"

I shake my head. "Did you learn that one from Matti?" Lacey's boyfriend, a doctor, has guardianship of his four-year-old nephew after a tragic accident left him all alone, and she's his nanny. Little Matti is just adorable, and I love when he comes into the Coffee Loft.

"Hey, don't knock it," she says, laughing. "Matti gets away with a lot just by poking that little lip out."

"I'm sure he does, ya big ole softy." I sigh and look around for an excuse. It's not that I don't want to be there for her, I just don't think I need to have input on her side of the business. My eyes finally meet hers, and I cave. "Okay," I say. "I'll come."

"Yay!" Lacey says, doing a little dance. Her excitement is contagious, that's for sure.

"I'll let you lead the way," Reid says, motioning for us to go ahead of him.

Lacey talks a mile a minute about her different ideas as we walk towards the front door. I'm laughing when, through the window, I spot a well-built man with a head of sandy blonde hair and broad shoulders across the street. My heart stutters in my chest. I don't know that I've ever had such a powerful reaction to a man before, let alone one I've only seen from afar . . . and across a street.

The handsome man turns, giving me a better view of his face. He looks so familiar. I squint my eyes and try to get a closer look. It looks just like a grown-up version of a twelve-year-old . . . *No way. It can't be!* My stomach knots in panic. This cannot be happening. Why is *he* here? He turns his head toward the café, and I drop to the floor on my hands and knees.

Please don't come in here.

I start to crawl out of the walkway when Reid, distracted by Lacey's chatter, snags his foot on my leg and goes down. Hard. Narrowly missing falling right on top of me by spinning around to land square on his bottom, his legs dropping heavily on my back.

"What in the world?" Lacey shrieks, spinning around and seeing us both sprawled out on the checkered linoleum. "What happened?"

"Oh my gosh, I'm so sorry!" I say, trying to assess the damage and wiggle out from under him.

Reid groans, moves his legs, and pushes to standing. "Aurora, are you okay? I'm so sorry, I didn't see you there." He brushes himself off, and pulls his suits coat sleeves down before reaching a hand out to help me up.

"What *are* you doing on the floor?" Lacey asks, her face a mask of confusion. "Are you hurt?"

"I'm fine," I say, frantically trying to think of a reason I'd be on the floor. "I thought I saw a piece of broken glass. Mr. Sanders dropped his glass yesterday, and you know you can never get it all." I take Reid's proffered hand, push to my feet, and brush my hands on my jeans. "Looks like it was a trick of the light." I risk a glance out the door and am relieved to see Gorgeous—I mean, Bradley is nowhere in sight. "Sorry about that, Reid."

"It's okay," he says, looking over the floor. "Is it safe to keep moving now?" His face reflects the confusion that's rioting in my head.

I nod. "Yep," I say, popping the p. "Let's go." *How can I be attracted to Bradley Jameson?* I shudder. *No way.*

Reid chuckles, the sound startling me. "It seems we're all jumpy today."

Lacey grins. "No more dropping to the floor without warning. You're gonna give someone a heart attack, or a broken neck."

I laugh, grateful for the tension to be broken. "Let's get back to work," I say. "We've got a dream to make come true."

Chapter Two

Bradley

Dirt kicks up from my tires as they crunch over the unpaved drive of the Lost Creek Construction office. The brick facade, designed to resemble that of a cozy home rather than a typical business, is warm and inviting. Built to be a replica of our most popular model home, it does well to showcase what our team can do.

I pull into one of the empty parking spots and climb out of the truck, a cup of the best coffee I've had in a long time in hand. The Coffee Loft was calling my name after I dropped into the bank, and who am I to refuse the call of caffeine? Besides, I figured I should try the little shop everyone's been raving about since I moved back to Piney Brook a month ago.

Plus, it's right next to the space we're looking at renovating for a customer. It would be great if my morning coffee was actually palatable.

I chuckle to myself and take a big swig of the Lofty Apple Cinnamon Latte I ordered. The guys would never let me live it down if they knew I liked the frou frou drinks. Their loss. The flavored coffee drinks are tasty. Not that I'd turn down a regular hot coffee with cream and two sugars, though.

"Morning," Allen says, when I walk into the office. "I've got a meeting this afternoon at two p.m. and I'd like you to sit in. It's for the reno job in Piney Brook."

I set my coffee on my desk and flip open the calendar. Another thing the guys give me a hard time about. Seems I'm one of the few men left who hasn't switched to a digital calendar. Usually, when I'm on a job site, I'm not scheduled for anything else. If I am, Cindy, Allen's assistant, calls me. "Should be fine. I'm writing up a quote for a potential client. Besides that, I'm good."

"Good," Allen says, dropping into the chair across from my desk. "Mr. Maxwell is bringing Lacey Chambers in to sign the contract for the build-out for the children's center. Reid went over this morning and should have the mock-up ready in time for the meeting."

"Perfect," I say, penciling the meeting in. "I can't wait until we get started over there and I can use my power tools. I hate pencil pushing."

Allen chuckles and stretches out in the chair, crossing his feet at the ankle, his fingers tapping a rhythm on his well-worn jeans. "Me too. We need this contract."

My eyes search his face. "Is there something you're not sharing?" I've been at Lost Creek Construction for the last two years. Recently, Allen split the north and south of Cobb County, putting Tim in charge of the crew in the north and me in charge of the one in the south.

When Allen suggested it, I jumped at the chance to take over the southern portion. I loved living in Piney Brook, a nearby town, as a kid and was itching to move back. Being in the southern part of the county more often gave me just the nudge I needed.

"Nah," Allen said, crossing his arms. "I'd just like to end this year with a big profit, maybe take the Mrs. on a cruise like she's been asking. This contract is just what we need to push the needle." He stands. "Plus, Mr. Maxwell has a lot of high-end connections. This could lead to more contracts for the company. Don't worry, your job's safe."

The phone rings from his office and he scuttles off to answer it, shutting his office door behind him. I hope he's telling the truth. I enjoy working for the man. He's got integrity, which is sometimes scarce in this business.

I hit the button to fire up the computer and review the preliminary information about the build-out. I'll get to the quote later.

☕   ☕   ☕   ☕   ☕

"Hey," Reid says, drawing me out of the trance I'm in. "Are you ready for the meeting?"

I sit back and stretch. "It's that time already?" The clock on the computer screen confirms it's 1:45 p.m. "Yeah, let's go."

Reid waits for me to lock my computer screen and come around the desk before starting off down the hall to the meeting room, his laptop bag slung across his shoulder.

"Don't you ever get tired of wearing suits?" I ask, taking in his pressed charcoal suit and tie. I'm comfortable in my jeans, polo, and steel-toed boots. Suits are too constricting. I can't imagine wearing one. Period. To my mother's dismay, I wore slacks and a button-down to my sister's wedding last year. No amount of cajoling could convince me to put on a monkey suit. It makes me sweat just thinking about it.

Reid laughs. "Just because you can't appreciate nice clothes, doesn't mean the rest of us don't." He pushes open the door to the conference room. A large dark wood table takes up the space in the middle. Comfortable chairs line the edges. Water bottles sit at each space, along with a pad of paper and a pen. At one end of the long conference table, Cindy has set up a dish with little packs of almonds and granola bars. "Allen is going all out for this."

Reid nods. "Mr. Maxwell has the potential to bring in a lot more business. We'll be in good shape for a long time if we can get his development company to do all their business with us."

Allen walks into the room and sets a tray with a pot of coffee, a small pitcher of cream, and a dish of sugar next to the snacks. "You boys get set up. They'll be here any minute."

"Yes, sir," Reid says, plugging his computer into the HDMI cord that'll project the screen onto the large TV mounted on the far wall. "We're all set."

"I'm going to escort them back," Allen says. He turns and walks out the door, muttering under his breath.

A few minutes later, a tap on the table gets my attention. "Here we go," Reid says, taking his seat and nodding toward the door.

"Reid, Bradley, I'd like you to meet Mr. Maxwell and Ms. Chambers."

Reid and I both stand and shake their hands. "Welcome," Reid says. "I think you'll be pleased with what I've drawn up."

Once everyone has taken a seat, he starts the slide show that outlines what the layout of the build-out will be, along with the connection to the current space next door. "Here, where you wanted some table tops, I've added outlets in the nearby walls in case patrons want to charge their phones or computers. And in each room, I've created a small space with a sink and a countertop. We'll do cabinets above for storage—open or with doors, your choice."

He continues, pointing out details he added as he drew up the plans. After showing the last slides, he asks, "What do you think?"

Lacey grins. "It's even better than I thought it would be."

"How realistic is this schedule?" Mr. Maxwell asks, looking over the contract Allen laid out with the timeline and budget listed.

"I'd say, provided we don't run into any early ice storms, it's realistic. As you can see," I say, reaching over and pointing to the chart, "we have built in a few extra days at each step for anything that may pop up."

Mr. Maxwell takes his time reading through the contract and passes it to Lacey. "I think it's a solid contract," he says.

Lacey reads through the papers and nods. "I see nothing on here we haven't discussed."

After a few minutes, they sign the contract, and we arrange a meeting to discuss the final plans next Monday morning at the Coffee Loft.

"Have you been there, yet?" Allen asks after walking Mr. Maxwell and Ms. Chambers out.

"I stopped in today before I came out here. The coffee was excellent. Have you?"

"No," Allen says. "Though, I've been meaning to stop in. That chain's supposed to be sourcing as many ingredients as they can locally." He shrugs. "Maybe I'll get over there once the renovation starts and try it."

"You should," Reid says, putting his computer back in his shoulder bag. "It's good." He chuckles. "Though the owner was a little . . . off this morning."

"Off?" I ask. "I didn't notice anything off when I stopped this morning."

"What time were you there?" Reid asks, powering down the computer.

"Around ten, I think. It was after I went by the bank."

"We must have been doing the walk-through next door."

"Oh." I'm going to be right next door for the next few weeks. I hope it's nothing to worry about. "What happened?"

"She seemed sweet before we got up to look at the space, then it was like she got spooked by something. She knelt to the floor, and I didn't notice in time to avoid tripping over her and fell on my butt, trying to avoid squishing her." He rubs his hand across his rear. "After that, she seemed jumpy as could be." He shrugs.

"Hopefully that was a one-off and she's easy to deal with. I don't want to go into the holidays with a stressful situation." I mentally cross my fingers. Last year, our clients were miserable, expecting us to work through Thanksgiving so they could host Christmas at their house. I had to remind them countless times their contract stated we'd be done by the middle of January. In the end, we finished midway through December. I think the guys were all ready to get out of there and enjoy their holiday.

"Well, I'm heading out. I'm meeting Briella for dinner." Reid swings his bag onto his shoulder. "I'll see you later."

"When are you going to ask that girl out?" Allen asks, pointing at Reid. "You know you want to."

Reid blushes. "She's just a friend."

Allen shakes his head, muttering something about taking chances as he walks out the door.

"I agree with Allen," I toss out. "You won't know unless you try."

He shakes his head. "It's better this way," he mutters as he follows Allen out the door, leaving me alone in the conference room. "Good luck on Monday."

Here's hoping the owner of the Coffee Loft isn't going to be a problem.

Chapter Three

Aurora

Beep beep beep. The sound of the garbage truck penetrates my dream and startles me awake. I open my eyes and am greeted by the bright morning sun streaming through the sheer yellow curtains of my bedroom window. Stretching my arms above my head, I wiggle my fingers and take a deep breath.

Wait! Sunshine?

I jump up, reaching for my glasses and knocking them off the table. *Not today!*

Gingerly, I slide out of bed and onto all fours, feeling around for the missing glasses. Figures I'd wake up late today. So much for being taken seriously. UGH!

Finally, my fingertips find the errant glasses. Snatching them off the floor, I slam them on my face and search for the alarm clock. The one I swore I set when I went to bed last night.

Six-oh-five. *Coffee beans!* I'm so late.

I rush to the kitchen and grab my phone from the charging station. I read it was bad to keep a phone near you when you're sleeping, leading me to create the cute charging station as far away from my bed as possible. Hence the old-school alarm clock that was *supposed* to wake me up—two hours ago.

I swipe the screen, pull up Lacey's number, and press dial. *Please let her answer!*

"Rory, where are you?" Lacey whispers. "I opened the shop, but you're about to miss the meeting with your . . . Hello, Mr. Maxwell. Right on time. Take a seat and I'll bring you some fresh coffee." Lacey pauses a moment, waiting for my dad to take his seat, I'm sure. I picture my dad, looking around the coffee shop—my coffee shop—wondering where I am. "Get here! I can't do this without you!"

I open my mouth to reply, but the click on the other end lets me know she's already hung up. I squeeze my eyes shut and take a big breath. Nothing to do but do it, right? I rush back down the hallway to my room. One glance at the closet, and I realize I've forgotten to swap the laundry loads. Perfect.

I snag a pair of jeans from the pile of "wear again" clothes on the treadmill in the corner that functions more as a second wardrobe than exercise equipment these days, and pull them up over my hips. Thank goodness I have a Coffee Loft polo still hanging in the closet. After yanking my hair into a messy bun, and brushing my teeth for two whole minutes, I slip on my shoes, grab my keys, and sprint to my car.

Ten minutes later, I pull open the door to the Coffee Loft. "Sorry I'm late," I start, looking around at the rest of the tables, which are blessedly empty of patrons. "I was . . . What are *you* doing here?" My mouth drops open. Blood rushes from my head to my torso, where my stomach feels like it's being weighed down by a box of rocks. *This cannot be happening.*

"Nice to see you again, Aurora." Bradley stands, reaching his hand out to shake mine. He gives me his signature smirk. The same one he used to flash when he teased me in the sixth grade. His dark eyes are twinkling with mirth. "I was wondering when we'd bump into each other."

I sputter. "What . . . Why?" Looking down at his outstretched hand, I do the right thing and place my hand in his before quickly jerking it back. Not before I felt a zing up my arm. I must have slept funny and pinched a nerve. Yeah. That explains it. I roll my shoulders.

"Oh, good," my father says, before taking a gulp of his coffee, not bothering to rise from his seat. "You two know each other. That should make this easy!" He grins. Blissfully unaware that this was the boy who caused his little girl to come home crying at least once a week in sixth grade. Well, indirectly, anyway.

Unease slithers down my spine when my brain registers what my father just said. "Make what easy, Daddy?" I ask, adding a touch of sugar to my tone. I may be an adult, but I'm still a daddy's girl.

"Bradley heads up the Lost Creek Construction team in Piney Brook. He'll be the one doing the build-out and connection for Matti's Playhouse and the Coffee Loft." He sits back and smiles. "We talked about that, remember? I wanted you two to use the crew I recommended."

I shake my head. "I mean, we talked about using Lost Creek Construction," I say. "I don't think you mentioned who would head up the project. I just assumed it would be . . ." I take a breath. "Someone . . . else."

Dad laughs. "After meeting Bradley when we signed the contract last week, I'm sure he's the right one for the job." He pats Bradley on the shoulder and takes a bite of donut, effectively closing the conversation.

"Great!" Lacey says, her voice a little too loud and squeaky. "Now that we have that worked out, let's go over the plan." She pats the seat next to her. "I saved you a spot, Aurora."

Realizing I'm stuck, I slide into the seat next to Lacey and put on my best face. I wrap my hands around the steaming mug of hot cocoa, the heat grounding me. "Sorry I'm late. What did I miss?"

For the next twenty minutes, I do my best to listen to the plans for the renovation next door. It's hard to concentrate, with Bradley eyeing me every chance he gets. His deep brown eyes sparkle in the morning light, and his dirty blonde hair is mussed like he's run his hands through it already. I mentally give myself a shake. I can't find him attractive. Not Bradley, the boy who tormented me in sixth grade.

"So, we'll need to barricade the area for the connection when we get to that step. Ideally, you'd close the shop for the day, but I understand that may not be possible." Bradley meets my eyes and waits.

"What? Oh, no. I'd like to stay open if possible. We get a lot of regulars, and I don't want to disrupt their routines."

He nods and continues. His words sound further and further away as I retreat into my own chaotic thoughts. His eyes meet mine, and he winks.

I thought he was cute in elementary school, but he's grown into a very handsome man. If I looked at him like that. Which I don't, thank you very much. Who cares if he has shoulders that look strong enough to carry three bags of coffee beans at a time? Or that he's got just the right amount of scruff on his chin to be attractive, yet not overly hairy.

I'm sure he's a bad kisser, though. There has to be something wrong with him. That thought brings a slight smile to my face, and I dip my head to hide it.

Suddenly, I wonder if he'll make fun of my hair again. Raising a hand, I smooth the mess that is my bun. If I hadn't overslept, I'd have taken more time to get ready this morning.

Oh, who am I kidding? A ponytail, jeans and a Coffee Loft shirt are my standard uniform. Why bother dressing in expensive clothes when I'm just going to spill drinks all over them? I sneak a peek at Bradley and my mind shoots me right back to the playground in sixth grade.

The replay of the first day he'd made my life miserable playing in technicolor in my head. *Bradley stopped me by the swings, reached out and grabbed my hair. "Your hair feels like my bunny," he said, a huge grin on his face. The girls in my class laugh and tease me mercilessly.*

"How does that sound, Aurora?" My dad's voice pulls me from my thoughts.

All eyes are on me as I struggle to recall what was just said. "Uh, sure." I blink away the tears pricking at the back of my eyelids and glance at Lacey, hoping that I've said the right thing. Her wide-eyed stare tells me I've missed the mark.

"Great!" Bradley says, beaming his thousand-watt smile at me.

I nod, pasting a pleasant look on my face. "Great."

"Well, now that's settled," Dad says, standing from his seat. "I'm going into the office. Keep me updated, won't you?"

Bradley stands and shakes my dad's hand. "Absolutely, sir. I'll walk you out."

"Let's go get the counter ready for customers," Lacey says, nodding her head to the counter. She gathers all the dirty dishes from the table and nearly sprints behind the counter.

"That's a good idea. I'll just check the water in the flower vases." The single gerbera daisy in each vase brings some added color to the space. I take my time and check each table before stepping behind the counter. I reach for my favorite cup and fill it with the nectar of the morning, a Mochaccino. The turquoise and beige mug reminds me of the beach trip I took last year. Closing my eyes, I visualize myself on the beach, toes in the sand, breeze in my hair. *Perfection.* "What do you think about getting a collection of coffee mugs with different designs and sayings on them for customers to use?"

"That sounds great," Lacey says. "Beats the plain white mugs we've been using."

"We could create a whole wall of mugs," I say, taking a sip of my coffee. "Maybe even have some to purchase. Coffee Loft merchandise . . . I like it!" Turning, I watch as Dad makes small talk while he waits for Bradley to roll up the plans and slide them back into a cardboard tube leaning against the wall.

"Okay," I whisper. "That didn't go too badly, though I wish they'd wrap it up and get out of here."

I sneak a good look at Bradley now that his attention isn't on me. He's too good looking for his own good. Every girl in elementary school had a huge crush on him. He could've focused on any of them, but no . . . he'd picked me as his target.

I turn to Lacey when I feel her staring at me. She meets my gaze, one eyebrow raised in question. "No," she says softly. "It went fine. Except the part where you were late and spaced out the whole time."

I cringe. "Sorry, I was surprised, that's all." Now that I've had some time to think about it, Bradley being in charge of the build-out is fine. I'm not in grade school anymore. Besides, he'll spend his time next door, and I won't even have to see his chiseled jaw or eyes like melted chocolate.

She nods. "So, you know Bradley?" A knowing smile teases her lips when she sees me staring again.

I finish the sweet drink in my mug before answering. "Yeah, I do. We went to elementary school together." I don't add that I'd actively avoided him anytime he'd popped up in town after that.

"Have fun tonight, Aurora." Dad winks at me before stepping out the door and onto the street.

Bradley smiles and lifts his hand in an awkward wave as he turns and follows my dad outside.

"What's tonight?" I ask Lacey, confused.

Her eyes dance with laughter. "Your dinner date with Bradley."

Chapter Four

WHAT A MORNING. I knew I'd run into Aurora again eventually. Or at least I'd hoped I would. Piney Brook is a small town, after all. I didn't expect it to be at a business meeting with her father. Mr. Maxwell had failed to mention who his daughter was at our meeting last week, and Reid hadn't given me a name for the owner either. Though, come to think of it, I should have guessed. Maxwell isn't the most common last name in town.

I grin remembering how flustered she was when she first entered the Coffee Loft. Her dark hair gleaming in the sunshine just like I remembered it. She took my breath away. If I believed in love at first sight . . . well, I guess it wouldn't be that since I knew her in elementary school.

She's always been quirky, and super smart. I had to stifle my laugh during the meeting, remembering how Reid had described her last week. Seeing her ruffled this morning makes me wonder if she's still the same fiery girl I was fascinated by as a kid. I wonder if she's ever thought of me over the years. I know I've been curious about her.

I had a serious crush on Aurora back in grade school. She sat right in front of me in class, her dark hair pulled back in a unique style every day, it seemed. She'd captivated me then, and if this morning is anything to go by, she's got my attention again.

My phone rings, and I hit the answer button on my truck's console. *Bluetooth connection for the win.* "Hello?"

"Hey, Bradley." Allen's voice rings out in the cab. "How'd the meeting go?"

Allen rarely joined for onsite meetings anymore, choosing to let Tim and me handle those.

"It went well. I think these clients will be easy to partner with." Although being so close to Aurora may not be as easy. I'm already longing for more time with her, to get to know the woman she's become. I suppose that's why I lost control of my mouth and invited her to dinner tonight. In front of her father and business partner. Not professional in the slightest, but the words were out before my brain could step in and put a stop to the madness.

"That's good news. We could definitely use a great contract to end the year. Did anything come up that might be a problem? Supplies or anything?"

My mind goes back to Aurora. Do I tell Allen I asked her out in the middle of a meeting? I probably should, but unlike before, my mouth's glued shut.

She was surprised to see me, but to be fair, I was surprised to see her as well. I was just better at hiding it. The silence carries on a bit too long, so I take a breath and answer. "No, sir. I think this project will be smooth sailing. I've got the supply list loaded. Everything seems to be in stock."

"Good. Let me know when everything's ready to go and you're starting the demo."

"Will do," I reply. "Reid's given me the official drawings, so I'll send everything in to get the permits rolling and complete the supply order."

"Sounds good. Listen, I've got to run. Cindy's motioning for me. See you later."

After saying goodbye, and hanging up the phone, I let my mind wander back to Aurora. She was always a go-getter, I shouldn't be surprised she owns a shop in town. In sixth grade, our teacher had each of us choose a business we'd like to run. We had to draw what it looked like and figure out what our products would be. I chose woodworking. I can't remember what Aurora picked, but I doubt it was a coffee shop.

She was smart, driven, and determined to make her way in the world. Even when the other girls teased her when they caught me staring at her. My mom said they were just jealous, so I ignored them. Mostly.

Until the day I saw Aurora wiping the tears from her eyes as she walked off the playground. I marched right up to Lauren and Miley and told them to knock it off. Of course it didn't do any good, but I had to try. They'd hurt my girl's feelings. Even if she wasn't really mine, I couldn't just let it go.

I rub a hand over my heart. I always considered her the one that got away, which is silly. We were kids, just out of the cooties stage. What did we know back then?

Though, now . . . who knows? Maybe now's my chance.

At least, I hope so.

Dinner tonight can't come soon enough.

          🌙 🌙 🌙 🌙 🌙

At four, I call it a day and head home. I'm still in disbelief that she said yes to going out to dinner with me. I'm really looking forward to getting to know her again tonight, but I'm also nervous. We've both grown and changed over the years.

What if she doesn't like the guy I've become? I didn't go to college and get a four-year degree. I don't spend my days in a fancy office or drive a fancy car. My house isn't mine, and I own more jeans and steel-toed boots than one man probably should.

I shake my arms and roll my head on my shoulders. The nerves are getting to me. I haven't had pre-date jitters in years. Maybe because no one has ever captivated me quite like her.

Aurora Maxwell, my first crush. I compared all the other girls to her, even after we moved to Lost Creek. I will never understand why we had to move forty-five minutes away. No amount of pleading or barricading myself in my room could convince my parents to stay in Piney Brook.

The first time I realized Aurora was special, we were in science class. Mr. Rupert was droning on about the planets. Listing them all off one by one. When he got to Uranus, one of the other boys snickered. Aurora had shot him a dirty look before promptly shouting, "Ur-uh-nus not Ur-ay-ness."

While everyone else in the class laughed and made jokes, one thought rolled around in my head on repeat—beauty and brains.

From that day on, Aurora Maxwell became someone I kept an eye on.

What are the odds that she'd be single—information her dad happily shared this morning waiting for her to show up for our meeting.

It's possible we will have dinner and the sparks I felt when we shook hands aren't there. I've built her up in my head for so long, I may not mesh well with the woman she's become.

Now that I'm pushing thirty, dating for the sake of dating seems like a waste of time. I would like a family of my own, and a wife to share my dreams with. Would she be interested in those things, too?

I pull into the driveway of my duplex and hop out of the truck. The small one-bedroom, one-bathroom apartment isn't the most elegant of homes, but it will do until I decide on a house to buy and make my own. I haven't found the right one yet.

I chuckle. The right woman, or the right house.

I toe off my boots at the door and make my way inside and through to my room. I shuck off my dirty clothes and hop into the shower. A half hour later, I'm standing in front of a mirror in a pair of gray slacks and a button up, wondering if this is dressy enough, or too dressy, for a sort-of first date.

I should have stayed behind and solidified our plans. Now, I'm second-guessing myself.

Why am I so nervous?

I smooth gel into my hair one last time, wash my hands, and grab my watch off the nightstand. I make my way down the hallway and into the living room. "Hey, Bagel," I say, scratching my cream, white, and brown cat on the head. "Did you have a nice day?" Bagel purrs and rubs his head against my slacks. I check his dish to make sure he has enough water, and give him a scoop of kibble. "I'll be back later," I say, wiping at the cat hair on my legs.

I take a deep breath and force myself to walk out the front door. Glancing at my watch, I realize I've got just enough time to stop by the little florist shop, Blooming Joy, near the Coffee Loft before meeting Aurora.

I stop on the front porch patting my pockets, mentally going over everything I need. A tip the school guidance counselor gave me when I was in trouble for forgetting to turn in my homework one too many times.

Nice outfit, check.

Phone, check.

Wallet, check.

Keys, check.

Breath mints, check.

I glance down at my feet . . . shoes . . . I need shoes.

I laugh and step back inside. *Who forgets to put shoes on?* Me, apparently.

Once I've slid into the nice pair of boots I reserve for meetings, church, and the occasional night out, I step back onto the porch, closing and locking the door behind me. "It's just dinner with an old friend," I say out loud to calm my nerves.

Truth is, in my heart, it feels like a lot more. It feels like everything hinges on this one moment in time.

Chapter Five

Aurora

"Mr. Sanders! So nice to see you. Would you like your usual?" I'm grateful for the distraction of the Piney Brook Gentlemen's Club, as I've dubbed them. The older men who come into the Coffee Loft on Monday and spend the afternoon gossiping about their wives, honey-do lists, and other town news.

He nods. "That would be great, dear. I'm just going to take a seat over here and wait for the rest of the guys, if that's okay."

"You bet. I'll bring your coffee right over." I rush behind the counter and begin making his drink, a hot coffee with enough cream to turn the whole cup nearly white.

"Don't forget, more milk than coffee," Mr. Sanders calls from across the room.

"You got it!" I chuckle to myself. If they only knew their wives gossiped just the same as they do when they meet here for a book club on Wednesdays.

"Here you go," I say, placing the hot cup of coffee in front of Mr. Sanders. "I've got some cinnamon rolls in the back. I'm going to heat them up. Want me to bring you one when they're ready?"

Mr. Sanders nods and takes a sip of his coffee. "That sounds great." He pulls out a newspaper and opens it to the sports section. One thing about the Piney Brook Gentleman's Club, they all like their physical newspapers. I thought everyone got their news online these days, but not these men. I asked about it once, and Mr. Walters said, "They can pry my paper out of my cold, dead hands."

I step into the back and glance up at the back wall where the big analog clock I picked up at a thrift shop in Pine Bluff hangs.

"If you keep glancing at the clock, time might stop," Lacey says from her place at the break table. "He won't be here until five thirty. Relax."

I shake my head. "That's just it. How do I tell him it was a mix up? I can't go out with *him*. I didn't even hear him ask!" I take the tray of cinnamon rolls and slide it into the toaster oven.

She laughs and pops a bite of raspberry pastry into her mouth. "You agreed, though. Your dad looked quite happy about the whole thing, too."

I shake my head. Of course, Dad would play matchmaker. He's been hinting more and more that he'd like to see me settled down. Thankfully, Mom seems to understand I'm focused on my career right now. She isn't pushing to have grandbabies in the next year, though Dad would be over the moon. "Do you think that's why he insisted on hiring Bradley?"

"No," she says. "Reid's the best architect in the county. Maybe even the state. So I'm sure Lost Creek Construction is top-notch as well."

"Oh," I say, frowning. Figures he'd be great at his job. Now I really don't have a reason to insist on using someone else.

Anyone else.

When the timer dings indicating the cinnamon rolls are warm, I take the tray out and set the rolls on a serving platter. "Better get these out there. I'm sure Mr. Sanders and the guys are wondering where I am."

Lacey nods. "I'll be out soon." She turns back around in the chair and stuffs the rest of her pastry into her mouth.

"Take your time," I say. "Don't choke."

At five o'clock, the dining room's cleared out. This time of night, we usually get a few high school kids who like to use the tables to study. I considered closing earlier, but I enjoy providing a safe place for them to get together.

"Are you ready for your dinner date?" Lacey asks, wiping the last of the dirty tables down.

"Uh, no." I look down at my clothes. "Why did you let me agree to this? You know I'm not good at dating. No one wants the girl who smells like coffee and couldn't be on time to save her own life."

"Here," she says, tossing me a t-shirt. "Put this on."

I duck into the restroom and swap shirts. "Seriously?" I ask.

"What? It's what I had in my bag." Lacey grins. "Besides, it's very on-brand."

I look down at the t-shirt, a giant coffee mug takes up most of the center. The phrase "Stressed, Blessed, and Coffee Obsessed" is splashed across the chest.

"I really don't think this is a good idea, Lacey. You know how my dates usually end. Awkwardly, with the man trying to get away as quickly as possible." Which is why I haven't bothered in the last few years. Why put myself out there, if it's just going to end badly, anyway?

"Knock that off. You're brilliant, amazing, beautiful . . ."

The bells above the door chime, interrupting her sentence. We both turn to greet the newcomer. "And brave," she says before grabbing the dish bin and scooting to the back.

"Lacey," I hiss loudly. "Come back here!"

When the only response is the swing of the pass-through door, I straighten and plaster a smile on my face. "Bradley, how lovely to see you again." He smiles and it feels like my heart stops beating. His eyes crinkle just a little, and it makes him even more handsome.

Stepping closer to the counter, Bradley pulls a bouquet of daisies from behind his back. "These are for you," he says, stretching his arm out and waiting for me to take the offering. "I noticed the flowers on the tables this morning, so I figured these would be a safe bet."

He noticed . . . *what now?* I didn't think men noticed much of anything, to be honest. My dad never seemed to notice when Mom added a new throw pillow or swapped out the living room rug. "Thank you," I say, taking the flowers from his hands. "You shouldn't have."

He cocks his head. "It's my pleasure. I'm just thrilled you agreed to go to dinner with me, for old times' sake."

"I'll put these in water," I say, turning to walk into the back. I need to get a grip.

"Whoa," Lacey says. "What happened?" She steps into the supply closet and comes back out, vase in hand. "Here, I'll do that. You talk."

I plop into the chair she was just sitting in and drop my head in my hands. "Lacey, tell me to grow up. Please? This is ridiculous. He can't come in here all gorgeous and smiling, and gorgeous, thinking I'm just going to let go of a year of bullying and tears." Heat creeps up my neck when I realize my eyes are wet.

"You said gorgeous twice," she points out. "Did he bully you?"

"Yes." I sigh. "No. I don't know. He would do things, or say things, and the other girls would run with it. They made my life miserable, Lacey."

She sets the vase with the colorful bouquet on the corner of the break table before taking a seat on the floor beside me. "Do you think he meant to hurt you? Or do you think those girls were just cruel and used his interest in you to fuel their nasty attitudes?"

I sit up in the chair, wiping my hands on my jeans. "The result is the same, right? Because of him, everyone called me Thumper . . . for months."

"Are you serious?" Lacey asks. "That's . . ." She slaps a hand over her mouth, trying to contain her giggles. "Kids can be so mean," she finally says. "Creative, but mean. Sorry," she says, when she realizes I'm not laughing along.

"I don't think I can do this," I say. Images of all the things that could go wrong flit through my mind like a grainy black and white movie.

She shakes her head. "I've never known you to shy away from hard things. You're the level-headed business woman. The woman who sees what she wants and goes after it. I'm surprised he's got you tied up in knots. I've never seen you this flustered over a man. Not even Jayme, who proposed to you, for goodness' sake."

"I know." My stomach knots. "I'm surprised, too," I say. "What do I do?"

Lacey smiles. "You have two choices. You can march out there and tell Bradley to jump off a cliff with weighted boots."

I gasp. "Lacey!"

She giggles. "Or you can go out there and show him you're stronger than you used to be. Go to dinner as a professional courtesy. Then you can avoid him like the plague if it's awful. I'll even bring you little satchels of potpourri to put in your pockets when he's next door. We'll call it Bradley repellant."

I laugh. "That seems extreme. How will some dried flowers keep him away from me?"

She shrugs. "Not sure, but during the black plague, people thought stuffing flowers in their pockets was a good idea. Can't hurt, right?" Grinning, she pushes up off the floor. "I'm going to check on Ashlan, and then I'm heading out. Knox is ordering pizza and we're watching the latest animated superhero adventure with Matti tonight."

I sigh. "Thanks, Lacey."

"No problem," she says, dusting her hands off on her pants. "I'll let Bradley know you'll be right out."

I nod. "Yeah. Thanks."

She stops as she reaches the door. "Who knows, maybe he's the man of your dreams."

She's gone before I can argue. I lean my head on the table and take a deep breath to gather my resolve. Today started off on the wrong foot, and I've been letting my emotions get the better of me ever since.

I'm going to this dinner, and I'll be the most professional business woman Bradley's ever seen.

Then, I'm going home, throwing that alarm clock in the trash and moving my phone back into my room.

Chapter Six

Bradley

I STARE AT THE swinging wooden door that now stands between me and an obviously distraught Aurora. Just before she turned around, her face had done that scrunch thing it used to do when she was upset. My mind races, trying to process what just happened. Maybe the flowers were too much? Is she seeing someone and her dad doesn't know? If so, why would she agree to have dinner with me?

I'm still trying to process the last few minutes when the door swings open again, and Lacey steps through. "She'll be right out," she says, stopping in front of me. She eyes me warily before placing both hands on the counter that divides us and leaning into my space. "Don't hurt her again."

"Again?" I ask, thoroughly confused. I hurt her? When? How?

"Thanks for waiting," Aurora calls as she steps through the doorway. "I'm ready when you are. I didn't have time to go home and change into anything more fancy, so . . ."

I glance between Lacey and Aurora. The air is filled with such thick tension, it's almost tangible. There's something I'm missing here, and I intend to figure it out.

"Jeans are good," I say. She runs her eyes over my outfit. "I wasn't sure what you'd be wearing. Better to be overdressed, my mom always said." I shrug. "I don't care what you're wearing, Aurora. It's a friendly dinner." She looks as beautiful as ever in her jeans and t-shirt. I almost chuckle out loud when I read what's on the front of the shirt, but I keep it inside, afraid to upset her more.

My eyes move back to her face in time to see her lips pinch together. Somehow, I think I've said the wrong thing.

Again.

"Ashlan, I'll be available by cell if you need anything."

"I'll be fine," the young woman says, before smiling at me. "I hope you two have a great time."

"Thanks for closing." Aurora turns to me. "Shall I follow you?"

Follow me? "I'd like to drive you, if that's okay. You've been on your feet all day. It's the least I can do." I hold my breath in anticipation of her turning me down. I get the feeling she's less than thrilled about this dinner date, and it makes my heart sink.

"Thank you. That's very nice of you. You'll bring me back to my car?" Her tone's more business than friendly. Hopefully, I can figure out what's bothering her before dinner's over.

"Of course," I say, stepping back and letting her lead the way outside. "I'm parked just over there." I point to a parallel space across the road where my truck sits. She doesn't respond, just looks both ways and crosses the street. I jog to her side of the truck and open the door. She may be wary of me, but I'm determined to be a gentleman.

"Thanks," she says, climbing into the seat. "You've got a nice truck." She blushes as her eyes find mine and my heart slams into my chest. Maybe she's not as immune to the chemistry I feel between us as she seems.

"It was the first thing I bought when I got my promotion with Lost Creek. I had an old Nissan hard body truck—Betsy. A hand-me-down from my uncle when I turned sixteen. While she was great for high school and when I was starting out, I wanted something a little nicer." I close her door and head around to climb into the driver's side.

"What happened to Betsy?" Aurora asks.

I grin. "She's in my parent's garage. I'm restoring her little by little. Maybe pass her down to my own kid someday." I shrug. "Who knows?"

"Oh." She tucks her hands between her legs. "So, where are we going?"

I start the truck and carefully pull out onto the road. "I thought we could go to Surfside."

She looks down at her jeans and t-shirt, a frown on her face.

"We have some time. Do you want me to swing by your house so you can change?" I ask, uncertain what she's thinking. "I've been to Surfside in jeans plenty of times, but if you'll be more comfortable in something else . . ."

She stares at me from her side of the truck, her eyes shimmering. Is she going to cry? How could this be off to such a rough start? I asked Tim and Reid, and they said Surfside was a great restaurant for a first date.

"Or," I say, thinking fast. "We can go to the pizza place up the road and grab a slice instead?"

"You've been to Surfside in jeans?" she asks.

I nod. "Yeah, I have. To be honest, this is the only pair of dress pants I own."

She glances down at my legs before averting her gaze.

"Really, Aurora. I don't mind getting pizza instead, or driving by your house. Whatever will make you more comfortable."

It looks like she's either deciding on something or giving herself a pep talk. Her lips are moving, but there's no sound coming out. It would be cute if I wasn't so sure I was already on thin ice.

"Let's get pizza," she finally says.

"Sounds good," I say, flipping on the blinker and taking the next right. "I like Pizza and Playtime more than Surfside, anyway." I glance her way when I feel her eyes on me.

"Then why were we going there?"

I shrug. "I wanted to impress you."

"Oh," she whispers. I dare to look over and see she's staring out the window.

The rest of the drive is quiet. The only sound in the truck is the soft music playing in the background. I keep searching for something to say, but I've got nothing.

I was hoping we would hit it off and all the fantasies I've had of sweeping her off her feet one day would come true. Instead, it feels like I'm lost in a country I've never been to and I don't know the language to ask for help.

Thankfully, Pizza and Playtime isn't too busy when we pull into the parking lot. At least we'll be able to get a table. I've no sooner parked the car than she's hopped out.

"Ready?" I ask, meeting her in front of the truck.

She nods. "You bet."

Okay . . . I open the door for her to step inside first. The noise of arcade machines is a drastic change from the near silence in the car. "What do you like on your pizza?"

She looks over the menu above the counter. "A Piney Brook Special sounds good."

I find that on the menu. "One Piney Brook Special, coming right up," I say. I wonder if I can pick mushrooms off the pizza without making it more awkward. I place our order and take the table tent from the young man who rang us up.

Aurora grabs the sodas from the counter and steps back. "Where do you want to sit?" she asks, looking around the nearly empty restaurant. I'm sure it's busier on a weekend, but I'm thankful it's not full of families and kids running everywhere right now.

"How about over in the corner there?" I ask, pointing to a quiet corner of the room, farthest from the games. Maybe we'll actually be able to hear each other and talk.

"Uh, sure."

I wait for her to lead the way, sliding into the booth opposite her and placing the table number on the edge.

"So, what brings you back to Piney Brook?" she asks.

I take my time unwrapping my straw and taking a sip of Coke to wet my parched throat. "Well, I really loved it here as a kid. I was upset with my parents for a long time after we moved."

She smiles. "I can understand that. I couldn't wait to get back home after college. There's something about Piney Brook that just pulls you in."

Conversation flows easily while we wait for our pizza to arrive. Finally, things seem to be going smoothly. When there's a lull, I take a deep breath and let it out slowly. "I was hoping to reconnect with you, actually." There, I said it. My heart is racing like I'm competing in the Olympics or something. I can't bring myself to look away from her.

Her eyes fly to mine, a startled look on her face. "Why?"

"It's always nice to reconnect with old friends," I say, back-tracking a bit. "Besides, I've been away so long, I wasn't sure you'd recognize me. When you did, I was pleasantly surprised."

"One Piney Brook Special," a young woman says, sliding the pizza onto the table between us and placing two plates beside it. "Anything else y'all need?"

"I don't think so," I say, watching Aurora.

"All right, y'all enjoy." The young woman spins on her heel and heads back in the direction she came from.

"How could I forget you?" she asks, her tone heavy.

"I'm sure I've changed over the years," I say. "Though you're still as beautiful as ever."

She blushes and tucks a strand of hair behind her ear. "You don't have to say that," she says, taking a bite of her pizza.

"I know I don't have to. It's true. You're just as beautiful as I remember you. All grown up now, but still as radiant. Your hair still shines in the light."

"My hair," she says flatly. "You always made fun of my hair."

"No, I didn't." I argue. I would've never made fun of her hair. It's one of the things I liked most about her. The deep chestnut of her hair always reminded me of the chocolate that we'd melt for s'mores in the summer growing up. Rich and smooth, it always seemed to glimmer in the sunshine. "I always thought your hair was pretty."

"Okay, let's change the subject," she says, ripping a bit of pizza from the slice and eating it.

She thinks I made fun of her? That I was no better than Lauren and Miley? My heart squeezes in my chest. No wonder Lacey had warned me not to hurt her.

Chapter Seven

Aurora

I MAY HAVE TO sit through this dinner, but I *do not* have to listen to him pretend like he wasn't at the root of all the bullying. I stuff the rest of the pizza in my mouth and pointedly look at my watch.

"I hate to cut this short, but it's getting late and I open the Coffee Loft in the morning." I force a yawn for good measure. "Ready to go?"

He's barely eaten a full slice, but I can't sit here anymore.

"Uh, sure. Let me get a box for the rest of the pizza. You can take it home with you." He pushes to his feet and heads to the counter where two teenagers are making moon eyes at each other.

From this angle, I can appreciate the slacks even more. They fit him snug across the bottom. Ugh! What is wrong with me? I rub my hands over my face. "Get it together," I whisper.

"What? I'm sorry, I didn't catch that." Bradley slides the uneaten pizza into the to-go box.

"Nothing," I say, grabbing my purse and sliding out of the booth. "Thanks for taking me back to my car."

He hesitates. "Aurora, I . . . Nevermind. You're welcome." He closes the box and motions for me to lead the way. At the truck, he opens the door for me to climb in before handing me the leftovers to hold. I wish he'd stop being so nice. This new grown-up version of Bradley is making it harder to remember why I don't like him.

The ride back to the Coffee Loft is tense, and I know it's my fault. I never should have agreed to this dinner to begin with. I wouldn't have if I'd been paying attention to the conversation when he asked. My head falls back to the headrest. I should have called and canceled when I realized my mistake. Lacey was so encouraging, and if I'm honest with myself, a part of me wanted to know what it would be like to spend time with someone as handsome as he is.

Lifting my head up, I sneak a glance at him. His jaw is twitching, almost like he's restraining himself from talking. Good. The less he talks, the less I'm charmed by him, and the easier it is for me to keep my walls firmly in place.

"Aurora," he says as he pulls into a parking space and puts the truck in park. "I'm sorry if I've done something to upset you."

I nod. "Thanks, but everything's fine." I slide out of the truck and close the door before he can say anything else.

The lights inside the Coffee Loft are shining through the windows, illuminating the parking lot. There's a table full of teenagers, textbooks spread out in front of them, laughing and carefree. For the first time, I am envious of people nearly half my age. Everything seems so easy for these kids.

After the trauma of sixth grade, I kept to myself through junior and high school. Too afraid to let people get close enough to hurt me again. Instead, I focused on my studies. I threw myself into school, and when Dad invited me to spend the summer with him at Maxwell Inc., I fell in love with business.

Of course, I tried dating a bit in college, but it was a bitter disaster. Hook-up culture had taken hold, and I wanted nothing to do with it. It was clear I was the prude in our college, and most of the boys quickly stopped even asking me out. Yet again, I felt out of place.

I refuse to feel like I don't belong in my own town. I'll have to figure out how to avoid Bradley, that's all there is to it. Easy peasy. I'll just stop thinking about how sad his eyes looked when I asked to leave the restaurant. Or how confused he seemed when I called him out for the bullying. Part of me wonders if Lacey was right, and he really didn't know how his words and attention fueled the flames from Miley and Lauren.

No. I will not feel anything for Bradley.

Attraction fades. I've seen it happen a million times. In fact, it's why I'm not married right now. When it came time to actually plan a wedding, I realized Jayme and I weren't really in love. We were comfortable, but there was no spark that would keep a marriage going. So, I'd called it off. Jayme had been relieved. Apparently, there was a new girl in his office that he fancied. Of course there was. No one chooses the chubby girl. Miley had been right about that all along.

It was true then, and it's true now. I just have to remind myself how badly I'd felt when the girls called me names and left mean notes in my backpack. Or how disappointed my parents were when I told them there wasn't going to be a wedding after all. That should do it.

After a fitful night tossing and turning, I give up at four in the morning and get dressed. Thankfully, I'd thrown a load of clothes into the washer and then into the dryer before falling into bed and praying for sleep.

Dressed in clean clothes, and with nothing to do around the house, I decide to head into the Coffee Loft early. Maybe I can create the new drink menu for winter. That's always fun.

Several hours, and many discarded attempts at new drink flavors later, Lacey and Matti walk in the door.

"Ms. Rora! Ms. Rora!" Matti calls as soon as he sees me. "Yacey said I can have a muffin and chocate milk!" He bounces on his little feet, trying to see inside the display case. "You have bueberry ones today?"

Lacey swoops him up, and he claps his hands. "You do!" He points to a big blueberry muffin with sugar on top. "That one, pease."

"For you, anything," I say, winking at him. I slip on a glove and grab the muffin he wants, putting it on a plate. "What about you?"

Lacey puts Matti on the ground, taking his little hand in hers, and points at an everything bagel. "Bagel with cream cheese and a vanilla latte please, the lofty size. Today I'm just going to caffeinate and hope for the best."

"Rough night?" I ask, popping her bagel into the toaster.

"I keep thinking of all the things that could go wrong, you know?"

"We've been over everything. Your projections look great, and the crew is getting started next week, right?"

"If they get the permits in time." She frowns. "What if we're delayed and I can't do my soft launch in December?"

"Then we kick off the new year with a bang!" I pass her the muffin and bagel. "You two have a seat and I'll bring your drinks over in a second."

"Thanks, Aurora." Lacey smiles and leads Matti to their favorite corner booth.

I make the drinks quickly and place them on a tray to deliver to the table. "Here we go," I say, placing Matti's chocolate milk in front of him first. "One chocolate milk fit for a king."

Matti giggles. "I'm not a king, silly. I'm a baseball boy!"

"Oh, I didn't know!"

Lacey sets a coloring book and a box of crayons on the table. "We just signed him up for t-ball."

"I'm gonna be the fastest baseball boy ever!" Matti exclaims before taking a huge bite of muffin.

"I bet you are," I agree.

Lacey takes a big drink of her latte, sighing as she sets it back on the table. "Thank you."

"No problem," I say as the door chimes with another customer. "I'll be back over in a minute." I ruffle Matti's hair and turn back toward the counter. My feet skid to a stop, nearly causing me to careen into a nearby table.

"Hello," I say, mustering my most professional voice. "What can I get for you this morning?"

Bradley's signature smirk is missing. In its place is a sad half smile. I don't like it. His eyes don't have the little laughter crinkles they do when he smiles for real.

"Hey, how about a hot coffee with cream and extra sugar?" He glances around the dining room. Spotting Lacey and Matti in the corner, he gives them a wave.

I nod. "You got it." Why is he here? He's not been to the Coffee Loft yet. Not for pleasure, anyway. Is it too much to hope he'd keep making his own coffee? "Decided to try out the coffee?" I ask, trying to fill the uncomfortable silence.

"I had some last week, and it was delicious. Figured I'd grab a cup this morning before I head down to the supply store."

"Oh, I didn't know you'd been in before." When was he here? With Lacey working less, I've been here open to close nearly every day.

He shrugs. "I didn't see you when I came in. Reid mentioned you were touring the space next door with him around the same time."

"Oh," I say, putting the top on his to-go cup and passing it across the counter.

"Listen, Aurora," he starts. "I get the feeling I'm not your favorite person. I'd like to know why."

I hand him his coffee. "It's on the house today."

"Thanks, but . . ."

"I'm sorry," I say, as another customer comes through the door. "More customers . . . I'm sure you understand."

He frowns, but nods. "Another time," he says.

I turn to the newcomer. "Good morning. How can I help you?"

Out of the corner of my eye, I see him stop at the table and say hello to Lacey. He must have said something funny because Matti's giggles carry across the room, making me smile. I'm sure Matti could make the grinch grin.

"Aurora," Mrs. Engles calls. "Did you hear me, dear?"

I drag my eyes away from Bradley. "I'm sorry," I say. "What was it you wanted?"

Mrs. Engles waggles her eyebrows up and down. "Easy to get distracted with a young man like that around."

I gasp, heat rising to my cheeks. "No, I . . ."

She laughs. "It's okay dear. I was young once, too. I'll take a cappuccino with a raspberry danish please."

I ring up her order, passing her the danish before turning to make her coffee. Once it's finished, I slide the mug across the counter to her. "Enjoy."

"Thank you, dear." She takes her breakfast to a table near the window, sets her things on the table, hangs her purse from the back of the chair, and pulls out a Kindle.

I wonder if I'll be eating alone in a little café when I'm her age. My mind skips to a picture of Bradley sitting across the table from me, sipping his coffee. Ugh, that man has gotten under my skin. I give myself a mental shake. This lady's obviously enjoying her morning. So what If I'm alone when I'm her age. She's healthy and happy. I hope to be so lucky.

"So," Lacey says, meeting me at the counter. "How'd it go last night?"

I cringe.

"That bad, huh?" She shakes her head. "He clearly has a thing for you. I could see it in the way he looked at you yesterday."

Could he really feel this attraction, too?

"He was a perfect gentleman. I had one slice of pizza and asked him to drive me back to my car." My shoulders sag. "I feel rotten about it, but I'm not sure why."

She gives me a sad smile. "I think it's time for a girls' night."

I shake my head and sigh. "Fine, you and Ashlan can come over and watch a chick flick at my house. Which night is best for you?"

"I have something a bit bigger in mind," she says, digging her phone from her purse. "Leave it to me. I'll set something up and get back to you. I've got to run. We need to get Matti his baseball gear." She leans over the counter and gives me a squeeze. "See you later."

I'm not sure how a girls' night will solve anything, but I've learned it's better not to argue with Lacey. She usually wins in the long run.

Chapter Eight

Bradley

"Hey, boss," Heath says, poking his head in the doorway of my makeshift office. "We're going to head out now. See you tomorrow?"

I lean back in the chair and rub my eyes with the heels of my hands. "Quitting time already?"

Heath laughs. "Already? We've been here nine hours. Not that you'd notice. You've been staring off into space with a goofy look on your face most of the afternoon."

"What, now?" I've been thinking of Aurora a lot today, but a goofy look? I doubt it. It's been five days since I tried taking her out on that date. Five days of walking by the Coffee Loft and peeking inside to get a glimpse of her. Five days of trying to figure out how to repair the damage I inadvertently caused her.

"I *would* say he met someone pretty," Hudson says from behind Heath. "But he'd have to go somewhere besides here and home for that to happen."

Heath shakes his head. "My money's still on a woman." He winks. "See you tomorrow, Bradley. C'mon, Hudson, Gabby's making lasagna and I'm sure there's enough for you, too."

"I've got plans," Hudson says, stepping into full view, his chest puffed out.

"Anne's going to be there," Heath says, a knowing smirk on his face. "But I guess I'll have to entertain them both alone."

Hudson sputters. "I guess I can make it."

I laugh as they both try walking out the door at the same time. They're not huge men, but big enough they bounce off each other like they're in a pinball machine.

Deciding to wrap it up for the day, I finish writing up the report that I promised Allen, and close up the computer. The cool autumn breeze washes over me as I step outside. There's a chill in the air tonight. I make a left instead of a right and head to the Coffee Loft. A warm cup of cocoa sounds great. Plus, a chance to see Aurora, since I noticed her car's still parked outside.

Just before I pull open the door, Aurora locks eyes with me . . . and swan-dives behind the counter. I laugh. That's a creative way to avoid talking to me. I'd be hurt, but I can't blame her if she really thinks I was behind the bullying. I only heard a little of what Miley and Lauren had said to her, and it wasn't good. I can't imagine what they said when I wasn't around to hear.

"Welcome." Ashlan, the barista who's usually working in the afternoon, greets me. "How can I help you?" She looks down to where I'm assuming Aurora is hiding on the floor, and back to me, a look of amused confusion on her face.

"I was hoping to say hi to your beautiful boss. Is she here?"

Aurora scoffs from her spot behind the counter. "Uh," Ashlan says, looking down at the floor behind the baked goods. "No, she's out for the night."

She glances back up at me and smiles. I admire her loyalty. "Hmm. I'll have to stop in another time, then. Can I have a hot cocoa please? Extra whipped cream and a dash of salted caramel if you have it."

Ashlan looks down again, clearly bewildered by her boss's behavior. "You bet." She rings up the order and takes my payment before stepping in a wide arch around where I'm assuming Aurora is hiding on the floor.

"When did you guys get all these mugs?" I ask, pointing to a rack of coffee mugs, each one different from the others. I chuckle when I see one that says. "Life happens, coffee helps." If that's not the truth, I don't know what is.

"Oh, Aurora thought it would be fun to add a mug display and let customers who were dining in choose a unique mug to use." She points at the rack. "That's what we've got so far."

"Neat idea," I say, taking the hot cocoa from her hands. "Thanks for this. Please tell Aurora that next time she doesn't need to dive behind the counter." I wink. "I won't bite."

I chuckle when I hear Aurora gasp. "See you ladies later."

⸙ ⸙ ⸙ ⸙ ⸙

A few days later, it's clear Aurora's still avoiding me. I work right next door. You'd think it would be easy to get five minutes of her time, but no. She's always busy with a project or a customer. I'm glad the Coffee Loft is so popular, but help a guy out here.

I would love nothing more than to ask her out again. Or at least figure out how to be on friendly terms without her diving behind furniture when she sees me coming. I shake my head. That was funny, but I'd like to get to a point where she's happy to see me. Or, at least, not annoyed by my existence.

"Hey, Bradley," Heath, the newest guy on the team, interrupts my thoughts. "I was going to run next door and grab some muffins and coffee. Need anything?"

Yeah, Aurora to talk to me. "I'll take some coffee. Thanks." I hand him the business credit card. "Use this."

I watch him leave and wonder if Aurora's next-door making coffee and small talk with her customers. Maybe I'll catch sight of her when I leave for the day. Somehow, I'm the guy who looks forward to little glimpses of a beautiful woman. I shake my head. Does that make me a creeper? I hope not.

I glance at the stack of wood left over from when we framed the rooms for the play areas and get an idea. Ashlan did mention a display for the mugs. There's a lot of wall space behind the cash register. I bet a wall display for the mugs would look great there. I could make that. Easily.

Then Aurora would have to talk to me. At least to say thank you. It's a flimsy plan, but it's all I've got right now so I'm inclined to go for it.

I open my laptop and start designing. Allen won't mind me using the leftover wood for this project. Usually, we donate it to the Re-New House thrift store in Lost Creek. I'll make a cash donation to their efforts in its place.

For the first time in weeks, I have a renewed sense of excitement. I can do this for her. It won't make up for all the times she was made fun of, but maybe it will show her I'm genuine and I actually care for her feelings.

"Coffee's here," Heath calls from the entryway. Hudson makes a mad dash to the muffin tray. "Any blueberry?" he asks.

Heath shakes his head. "I don't know. I just asked for a few muffins." He puts the box of muffins and the container of coffee on the makeshift break table and steps back. "Help yourself."

Hudson's already digging into a muffin. "Delicious."

I laugh. "You're a mess, Hudson." I make myself a cup of coffee, adding creamer and sugar from the Tupperware container we keep on the table. "Finish up and get back to it. We need to complete the framing this week, so we stay on target."

He nods. "You got it."

The phone rings and I step outside to answer it. "Hello?"

"Hey, Bradley, I have a potential client who wants to look into renovating the old bank building in Piney Brook. Think you can meet him there this afternoon and get a feel for what he wants?"

I turn and look through the glass-paned doors at Heath and Hudson as they finish eating and pick up their tools. "Shouldn't be a problem. Do you have a time in mind?"

I'm leaning against a bench just outside the Coffee Loft when I spot her. The rich caramel color of her hair pulled high into a ponytail, and her radiant smile as she helps a customer, stop me in my tracks. My heart lurches in my chest.

I force myself to turn around and look away while Allen continues to fill me in on the details for the meeting.

"Thanks for taking this on while you're in the middle of another project." Allen pauses. "I still mean to get down there and try some of that coffee I've been hearing so much about."

At the mention of the Coffee Loft, I turn back around, just in time to see Aurora's face pinch in distress. My feet are moving before my brain has time to react.

I pull open the door, the tinkle of the chime alerting her that someone's stepped inside.

"Well, well, well," the customer at the counter says as she turns around and faces me. "If it isn't Thumper and Bambi."

I stop. "Miley, what a surprise." And not a good one. Even after I left, I heard stories about her and her girl crew's antics. Seems they'd bully anyone who dared be different than them. From the looks of it, not much has changed. "What brings you to Piney Brook?"

"I'm in town visiting my parents for a while, and they told me our little Thumper opened her own coffee shop. I just had to come down and see for myself," Miley says, her voice dripping with contempt before she turns her fake smile at Aurora. "Seems some things never change, no matter how old you are."

She gestures her hand up and down in front of Aurora. Implying what exactly, I'm not sure. Miley can't possibly mean there's something wrong with Aurora's body.

I risk a glance at Aurora. Her cheeks and neck are flaming red. Tears glisten in her eyes. "Hello, Bradley," Aurora says, her spark gone. "Miley was just about to order and go." Aurora glares at Miley, showing a bit of the backbone I've come to expect from her.

"Can I get . . . whatever you serve here that doesn't taste awful?" Miley slaps down a five-dollar bill, then turns and glares at me. "What are you doing here? I thought you moved away from this small town and its . . . limited options."

"I'm back. I'm working next door and stopped in to tell Aurora how thankful I am for her tasty coffee and delicious muffins. It's been keeping me and the guys motivated." That's not entirely untrue, but I'd hoped to discuss how we might move on from the past. "There's nothing quite like a Coffee Loft coffee to brighten the day." I raise a brow and hope she can take a hint. Her vitriol is not welcome here.

"Aww, isn't that sweet," Miley says, and rolls her eyes. "Seems someone still has a crush on the chubby girl. Though, I do wonder what's wrong with you . . . since you're still single and all."

Aurora's hands shake as she hands Miley her coffee—in a to-go cup. "Here you are. Black coffee," she says, her voice cracking as she talks. My heart aches for her. Miley must have been even worse to her after I moved for it to still be affecting her all these years later.

"Too bad Bradley didn't stick around and see you in high school," she shudders. "The braces were really something." Miley takes a sip of the coffee and sighs. "I suppose it will do," she says. "It was a pleasure to see you both." She spins on her heel and stomps out the doors. That was . . . interesting.

"Aurora . . ." I start, but she holds up a hand and cuts me off.

"Thank you for stopping in," she says, curtly. "I'd appreciate it if you'd send someone else next time." She blinks rapidly, as if holding back her tears.

"I'm sorry, what?" I'm as stunned by what just happened as she is, but she can't be serious.

"Every time you're around, something bad happens. Please, just stop." She turns and rushes through the door to the back room.

Well, that didn't go as planned.

Chapter Nine

Aurora

Of course, Bradley would be here when Miley Becket stops in. She was the ringleader of the Make Fun of Aurora Club. My mom had said seventh grade would be a fresh start, and I believed her. Especially when Bradley's family moved away. A new, bigger school, a chance to make new friends . . .

Turns out, seventh grade didn't bring the relief I'd so desperately wanted. All the kids from Piney Brook Elementary got funneled to the same junior high school in Barberville. Which meant Miley and Lauren kept up their taunting, but now they'd recruited *more* friends to help make my life miserable.

I furiously swipe at the tears running down my face. I am a grown woman. This is ridiculous. A silly childhood bully shouldn't be getting me so worked up. I'm a successful business owner. She's probably married to a snooty lawyer who is just as awful as she is. That thought makes me smile.

Ugh, I'm no better than her.

Great. My momma would be so disappointed if she knew I was thinking ill of other people.

I take a breath and step into the bathroom to splash water on my face and notice my red-rimmed eyes in the mirror. Maybe it's time to employ those affirmations my high school guidance counselor taught me about.

I pat the water off of my face. "You are smart. You are strong. You are beautiful. You are unstoppable. No one can ruin your day."

Yeah . . . right. I've always been too pudgy, too fair skinned, too busty, too . . . too something. And girls like Miley, who seem perfect from the outside, never missed an opportunity to let me know. Apparently, they grew up to be mean women, too.

Tossing the paper towel into the trash can, I hurry back out to the front. Lacey officially resigned last week, and Ashlan doesn't come in until later, leaving me the only one here. I make a mental note to hire more part-time staff.

"Aurora, dear, what's wrong?" My mother rushes around the counter and pulls me into her arms. "I stop in for coffee and find you looking like you just cried your eyes out."

I let her hold me for a minute, finding comfort in the familiar touch. "I'm okay," I say, stepping out of her arms. "Just a rough morning."

"Did a customer yell at you?" She searches my face.

I duck my head. "Miley Becket stopped in for coffee." I grab a towel and wipe the already clean counters.

"What did she say to you? I'm going to have another talk with her mama." Mom's face is red with fury. "I've had just about enough of those ole Becket biddies."

"What do you mean, 'another talk?' Mom, please . . . tell me you didn't." She wouldn't have. I asked her to stay out of it. Even back then, I knew getting my mom involved was the worst of bad ideas.

"Well, someone had to do something. That little girl made you cry all the time." She harrumphs.

"Please, please promise me you won't say a word to her, her mother, or anyone else for that matter. I'm a grown woman. I can handle a rude customer. It's part of the job." I sigh. "Promise me."

"Fine." Momma smooths down her dress and pats her perfectly coiffed hair. "How about a coffee to go, and a muffin. Throw one in for your father, too, if you don't mind. He'll love that."

I gather everything together and hand it to her. "I love you, Mom."

She pats my hand. "I love you, too. You just let me know, and I'll march right over to Mrs. Becket's house and give her a piece of my mind."

I laugh, feeling light for the first time in the last hour. "I will."

She nods her head. "See you later, dear. I'm off to get a pedicure."

Mom steps out the door, and it's like she opened the floodgates. Several customers enter at the same time, all looking harried and impatient. The line never seems to end. As soon as one customer leaves, another steps inside and stands in the back of the line.

The steady stream of customers keeps my mind off of Miley and Bradley. I'm thankful for the influx of patrons. This time last year, I was nervous the Coffee Loft might not take off. The marketing efforts I've put in place the last six months seem to be doing the trick, since nearly everyone is buying the special of the day.

"Hi, Aurora," Ashlan says, as she scoots behind the counter and slips her apron on. "Seems like you've had a busy afternoon."

"We've been steady," I say, wiping up a pile of coffee grounds from the back counter. Things finally slowed down a bit about twenty minutes ago. "I'm thrilled."

Thankfully, she hadn't questioned my craziness when I'd hidden from Bradley behind the counter the other day. She'd just gone with it. Though I could see the question in her eyes. Ashlan deserves a raise for putting up with the insanity that is Aurora Maxwell these days.

She points to several dirty tables. "I'll clean those first and then see what else you need."

I watch as she grabs the towel and a dishpan and starts clearing the tables. Ashlan's really stepped up since Lacey resigned. With all the changes, I'm grateful to have her on my team.

"Ashlan," I say when she comes back behind the counter to put the dish bin away and wash her hands. "How would you feel about more hours?"

She squeals. "Seriously? I'd love that."

"I'm thinking I'll need an assistant manager. I'd like you to consider the position."

She gapes at me. "Assistant manager?"

I nod. "Yes. It would mean more hours, and more responsibility. It would also mean a raise. Now that business is picking up again," I say, nodding to the dining area, "I'm in a position to make the change."

"I'd love to," she says.

"Great, I'll get everything in order, including a job description and a contract. We'll be even busier when they're done next door, and I'm hoping to hire a few part-time people to help us out. If you know anyone, send them my way."

She grins. "I will. Thanks for this!" She hugs me.

"You deserve it," I say. "I have to do the weekly order, so I'll be in the back if you need me."

She waves me off and gets started making a fresh pot of coffee. "I've got this."

I look around the space one more time, pleased at the number of tables that are filled at this time of the afternoon. People are scattered around the room enjoying their coffee, reading or on their computers, and it makes me smile. Before I head to the back to my little office, I snag a muffin and refill my coffee.

I've just finished the purchase order and I'm writing up the contract for Ashlan when my phone rings. "Hello?"

"Hey," Lacey says, sounding out of breath.

"Are you running?" Lacey never runs.

"Ha!" she shouts. "You know better than that. I just walked up the hill to the baseball field where Matti's having his first practice. I need more cardio in my life."

"Aren't you allergic to cardio?" I ask. She's been trying to get in shape since before she and Knox started dating. I know she wants to look her best for her wedding, even if Knox tells her she's perfect just as she is. Who am I to argue? We all have our insecurities.

"Yeah, I am, but if all his practices and games are up this hill, I'll be fit in no time." She chuckles. "Anyway, I was calling because I've spoken to the girls, and we all agree that Saturday night after the Coffee Loft closes is the perfect time for a girls' night. I'm bringing clay face mask stuff. Ashlan's going to get some sodas and sparkling water, Anne's bringing some deep conditioning treatments for our hair, and I've even got Karlee and Briella coming."

"Uh, that many people?"

"It will be fine. These are great women, you know that. Plus, you need some time to primp and do things that make you feel good about yourself."

I hesitate. I don't know most of the women she listed very well. Of course I've seen them around town, and I've met them a few times when they've come in for coffee, but I don't *know* them, know them.

"Don't overthink it," Lacey says, as if she's read my mind. "See you Saturday." She hangs up before I can think of an excuse she'd believe.

Looks like I'm having a girls' night.

Chapter Ten

"Mom," I say when she answers the phone.

"Good to hear your voice," she says. "You don't usually call me in the middle of the day. Everything okay?"

I take a deep breath. "Do you remember Aurora Maxwell?" Her joyous giggle catches me off guard.

"Do I remember Aurora? Of course, dear. She was your first crush. Poor thing, you were in knots about her." She chuckles. "Have you seen her?"

I shake my head. Of course Mom would find delight in how tangled up I was over Aurora. "I have. She's the owner of the Coffee Loft in town."

"Oh," she says, her tone softening. "The one you're renovating?"

I sigh and rub my hand through my hair. A habit I've not been able to break since grade school. "No. Well, kind of. We're working on a build-out of the space next door, but we will connect the two businesses soon. Probably next week once we finish the framing and drywall."

"Well, that's nice." She waits. Mom's always been good at waiting for me to spill my guts. I wonder if that's a skill moms get during pregnancy. Is it part of the package? Like eyes in the back of their heads or something?

"It is. It would be. I don't know, Mom." I frown when I remember the way Aurora's hands shook passing Miley her coffee. "It seems she blames me for being bullied." Mom's shocked gasp makes me feel a little better.

"Bradley Paul Jameson, you better not have bullied that girl."

I pull the phone from my ear. Is she serious? "Mom, you know I'd never, ever bully anyone." I shake my head. "Apparently, some things I said to her, in a misguided attempt to get her attention, were used against her by some mean girls at school."

Mom huffs. "Then why does she think it's your fault?"

I sit on the bench outside and take a deep breath of the cool afternoon air. "I don't know. She shuts down every time I try to talk to her, but that's not the worst part."

Mom groans. "What could be worse than that?"

I relay the details of Miley's surprise visit.

"Wow," Mom says when I'm done. "That's just mean, and she asked you to stay away?"

"She did. What can I do? I would really like the chance to get to know her again." If Mom can't help me, I'm really out of luck. Mom doesn't answer right away, and my nerves kick up another notch. "Mom?"

"I'm here. You're not going to like this, but I think you should respect her wishes."

"But . . ."

Mom cuts me off. "No, son. You respect that woman's wishes. If she doesn't want you coming into her coffee shop for a while, give her space. Find other ways to show her you care."

My shoulders slump in defeat. "You're right. I just don't know how."

Mom clicks her tongue. "You'll figure it out. If she's worth it, you'll find a way."

"Thanks, Mom," I say, lifting my head and looking through the window into the Coffee Loft. "I'll start thinking on what to do. I've got to run. I have a meeting soon."

"Keep me posted. I love you."

"Love you, too, Ma." I hang up and slide my phone into my back pocket. The weather's beautiful today, so I decide to walk the few blocks to the old bank building to meet Caleb Miller and see what he has in mind.

The downtown streets of Piney Brook are lined with brick storefronts. Huge display windows hint at what's inside each one. I pause outside the florist shop. A huge bouquet of fall-colored flowers draws my attention. They are beautiful, but not nearly as beautiful as Aurora.

Wow, when did I get so sappy?

Checking my watch, I see I have a few more minutes to spare, so I pop inside the flower shop.

"Hello," an older woman with flowers in her graying hair greets me. "How can I help you today?"

I point to the flowers in the window. "Do you think you could make three big bouquets like that with Gerbera Daisies?"

The woman smiles. "Let me check my stock." She slips through a door at the back of the room. She's gone for just a few moments before coming back. "I should be able to do that if you don't mind me adding a few other things to fill it out."

"That would be perfect, thanks."

She gets out an order pad and starts writing up the order. "Special occasion?"

"No, just a special person."

She smiles and slides me a card. "For your personal message," she says.

I grab a pen from the cup on the counter and pause. What could I say to let her know how I feel?

After filling out the card, I pass it and my debit card to the woman. "Thanks so much for this."

She chuckles. "Thank you! I'll make sure these are delivered this evening." She gives me the debit card back and pats my hand. "I'm sure she'll love them."

"I . . . Thanks. I hope so." I say goodbye, step back out onto the sidewalk, and hurry along to the old bank building, arriving just in time for my meeting.

"Caleb?" I ask, as I approach a gentleman standing in front of the doors.

"That's me," he says. He's dressed in dark navy scrubs with "Dr. Miller" embroidered on the breast pocket.

We shake hands. "Nice to meet you. I'm Bradley Jameson. Allen told me you wanted to discuss a project. What did you have in mind?"

Caleb opens the door and steps back for me to enter first. "I'm moving back to Apple Blossom Ranch, and I'd like to open a veterinarian office and grooming space here in town. I know the Cobb County Animal Shelter is offering some basic care, but to get to a more comprehensive office is a bit of a drive."

I nod, turning around in a circle to take in the space. "So you'd like to split this space in two?"

"I was thinking something like thirds with two-thirds being the vet space, and a third for a grooming area." He steps to the side. "I'd like to have the front open to both, so we could leave that counter for the office staff." He points to the existing counter space. "Here would be a waiting area, and then I'd like two or three exam rooms, and a surgery area in the back. The rooms would need to open to the back, and to the front."

I make notes on my phone while he talks. "This all seems doable. Would you like to hire someone to draw up the plans?"

Caleb stuffs his hands in his pockets. "I was hoping you'd have a recommendation."

I nod and shoot him a friendly smile. "I do. I'll send you Reid Douglas's information. He's who we usually recommend."

"Thanks," he says. "So, do you think it's realistic?"

I take a minute to look around. The space seems large enough to me. "I think so. Let's get Reid in here and see what he thinks."

Caleb lets out a relieved breath. "Thanks, man. I appreciate it. My brother thinks I'm nuts and would rather I set up shop at the ranch, but that's just not realistic."

"Where is Apple Blossom Ranch, if you don't mind me asking?" I'd seen some jars of jam set out at local stores, but I didn't realize it was close to Piney Brook.

"Just outside of town, on the way to Barberville. Closer to Barberville, honestly, but Piney Brook's charm is hard to resist."

I nod. That's not the only thing in Piney Brook that's hard to resist.

After our meeting, I decide to text Tim.

> Up for meeting me at McFadden's for a burger?

I've got to do something. Otherwise I'll be sitting outside the Coffee Loft waiting for the flowers to get delivered and I will officially be a creepy stalker. Not a good look.

> Sure. Five okay?

I glance at the clock. It's 4:15, that should be plenty of time.

> See you then.

I walk back to the job site. Looks like the guys have packed it up for the day. With as early as we usually start, I don't blame them for being ready to go at four. Besides, they made good progress today.

After cleaning up my makeshift desk space, and checking to make sure it's all locked up, I hop in the truck and head toward Lost Creek and dinner.

The parking lot is packed when I pull in. That's what I get for trying to go out on a Friday night. I see Tim's truck in the lot. Hopefully he's got us a table. I find a space and hop out. The gravel crunches under my boots as I make my way to the big wooden doors. Once inside, I let my eyes adjust to the dimmer lighting.

"Can I help you?" a pretty woman, probably in her early twenties, asks.

"I'm meeting a friend," I say, looking around. I spot Tim in the corner waving his arm. "I think I just found him, thanks." I step around the hostess stand and make my way through the tables to the booth in the back. "Hey, man. Thanks for meeting me."

Tim grins and passes me a menu. "No problem. It's been a while since I've seen you. Piney Brook keeping you busy?"

Tim and I used to meet up for dinner a couple times a week. Both single, and neither one of us interested in dating, we clicked and kept each other company. "Yeah. This project's been interesting, that's for sure."

The waitress approaches the table and takes our orders. Tim watches her walk away, shaking his head slightly. "I knew her in high school," he says quietly. "I always figured she'd leave town and never come back."

I glance in the waitress's direction. "Sometimes home is better than anywhere else." I shrug. "I moved back to Piney Brook because it's where I always felt the most at home, you know. Maybe when push came to shove, she realized she didn't want to leave."

Tim sighs and leans back in the booth. "Yeah."

He's quiet. "You okay?"

He looks up from where he was staring at his water glass. "Yeah. So, what's new? Met anyone interesting since you moved?"

I must make a face, because suddenly, he's leaned forward and is interrogating me.

"Okay, let's hear it. I need her name and how you two met. Is it someone I might know?"

I hold my hands up in surrender. "Okay, okay, you got me."

The waitress comes back to the table and drops off the sodas and burgers we ordered. "Thanks," I say before digging in.

Tim waits for me to finish my bite. "You gonna spill, or what?"

I shrug. "Or what."

He shakes his head. "All right, but when you're ready to talk, I'm ready to listen."

I laugh. "Thanks man." I take a look at the time. Aurora should be getting her flowers about now. I just hope she likes them . . . and the message.

Chapter Eleven

Aurora

"Aurora," Ashlan says, pulling my attention from the schedule I'm working on. "You need to come see this."

I groan. "What happened?"

"Uh," she hesitates. "It's not bad . . . just . . . a lot." She giggles. "There's a delivery here for you."

"Okay, I'm coming." I follow her to the front where a person—I can't see if it's a man or a woman—is holding a huge display of gerbera daisies. "What on earth?"

"Ms. Maxwell?" The flowers move to the left, revealing a petite woman.

"Yes, that's me," I say, glancing behind her at two other vases filled with colorful flowers sitting on a nearby table.

"These are for you." She passes me the bouquet she's holding. "Have a great day."

I bring the flowers to my nose and inhale the lovely scent.

"Where'd all these flowers come from?" Mr. Sanders asks as he and Mr. White approach the counter. "Looks like the flower shop threw up in here." He shakes his head and sneezes, then shuffles further away.

"I think someone's sweet on our Rory," Mr. White—Steve—says, looking at the flowers on the table. "Wonder who it could be."

"No one is sweet on me," I say firmly. "I'm sure my parents sent them. My birthday's coming up, you know." Though, why would they send so many?

"I don't think so," Mr. White says, holding a card up and grinning. "Unless your parents think these flowers aren't as beautiful as you, and they're named Bradley." He chuckles and passes the card to Mr. Sanders.

"No, Aurora." Mr. Sanders says, grinning like the Cheshire cat. "Someone's definitely sweet on you."

Ashlan giggles. "Wow, no one's ever sent me flowers at all. Let alone three huge bouquets at once. What do you want me to do with them?" she asks.

Mr. Sanders hands me the card. "Move them to the break table for now," I say. "I'll figure out what to do with them from there." I slide the card into my pocket to look at later. "Gentlemen, what can I get you this evening?"

After delivering their orders, two decaf cappuccinos and a slice of pumpkin pie for each of them, I dip back into the office.

Reaching in my pocket, my fingers graze the card and pull it out. I glance down at the card in my hand. "Piney Brook Florist" is written in swirly font, with a bunch of flowers in the corner. I flip it over and read.

These flowers may be beautiful, but they pale in comparison to your radiant beauty. You light up every room you enter. Never let someone steal your shine. They aren't worth it. Bradley

The beating of my heart drowns out any noise from the coffee shop. I've always thought of Bradley as the enemy, not someone who cares how I feel. Except, every time I push him away, or assume the worst, he shows me a different side of himself. One that I hadn't expected to see. One that I am finding hard to resist.

What do I do now?

☙ ☙ ☙ ☙ ☙

Saturday afternoon, I leave Ashlan and the new part-time girl Bexley to close while I go home and get ready for company. I'm pulling into Harvest Pantry, Piney Brook's grocery store, when I notice Bradley's truck parked in the space closest to the doors. I groan.

Do we really need snacks?

I still don't know what to think about the beautiful flowers, and that message . . . That was sweet. What do I say now? *I'm sorry I misjudged you all these years? I think you're handsome?* Ha! No way.

Besides, I'm still the chubby girl who isn't into dating for the sake of a quick hookup. That part hasn't changed, and guys don't seem to want that kind of girl. Or, at least, they don't want me. Not forever, anyway.

Deciding there's no way around it, I find a parking space and head inside. I'm just grabbing popcorn, chips, and a fruit bowl. What are the odds I'll bump into him, anyway?

I spot Miley and Lauren in the produce section, and slide my cart further behind a huge display of toilet paper. Yes, I'm hiding from the mean girls—it'll make my day simpler if I don't have to deal with them.

"Aurora," a deep voice calls from behind me. I jump, slamming the cart into the display and causing the mountain of two-ply to come toppling down. Laughter rings out from nearby, and I swing my head toward the sound.

If the ground could open up and swallow me whole now, that'd be great. Bradley appears next to me and starts grabbing packages of baby-soft toilet paper off the floor. Miley Becket and her BFF Lauren have come over and are both snickering and pointing at the disaster that is my life. How is it possible I run into all of them at the same time? If only there was another grocery store in town, I'd have a fifty-fifty chance at avoiding unwanted company.

Who am I kidding? I'm not that lucky.

"Here, sir. I've got it. Happens all the time." The squeaky voice of a teenager coming to Bradley's rescue makes the whole situation seem infinitely worse. Why couldn't a grandmotherly woman have come to help?

"I'm so sorry," I stammer. "I can help clean it up."

The teen shakes his head. "No, ma'am, I've got it. Thanks."

"Oh. Okay. Thank you for doing that." I stand awkwardly, not sure what to do now.

"Come on," Bradley says, putting his handful of things in my buggy. "Let's go get your groceries."

I nod meekly. "Thanks." He points to the produce section. "Want to start there?"

I shake my head. "No. Let's go get some chips and popcorn."

He turns the cart back around and starts walking toward the snack aisle like we're not leaving the great TP avalanche of '24 behind us.

"Don't worry about it," he says when he sees me looking behind us for the tenth time. "I'm sure that happens a lot. I once heard tell of a shelf full of laundry detergent exploding across the whole store. It was so slippery, nobody could walk—they had to swim out."

I giggle. "That can't be true."

He shrugs his broad shoulders. "It got you to laugh, though." He turns the cart down the snack aisle and stops near the popcorn. "Which kind did you want?"

"Why are you being nice to me?" I blurt, slapping my hand over my mouth the minute the words are out.

He laughs nervously. "Well, I'm sure it's no big secret that I had a crush on you in grade school."

My jaw drops.

"Okay . . . I guess it was a secret, then," he says, pointing to a box of popcorn. "That one okay?"

"You what?" I ask, my voice barely above a whisper.

"You had to know," he says. "I complimented you every chance I got."

"You weren't trying to make fun of me?"

He drops the box of popcorn in the cart and gently grabs my face, one hand on each side of my jaw. "Aurora Maxwell, you were the brightest, most beautiful girl I'd ever seen. I'd never, ever make fun of you. I didn't know how to just tell you I liked you back then, so I thought complimenting you and being around you as much as I could would give you a hint. I am so sorry you were ever bullied because of it."

"You liked me?" I ask again, unable to comprehend this twist of events.

"I liked you then, and I like you now. Why do you think I've been trying to get your attention? Apparently, old habits die hard." He rubs his hands through his hair. "I'm telling you, right now, Aurora Maxwell. I like you. I'd like to be your friend. More if it's possible."

He likes me. My heart feels like it might explode. *Bradley Jameson really likes me.*

When I don't respond, he takes my hand and keeps moving down the aisle. "What are we stocking up on snacks for?"

"Oh, girls' night," I say. "Lacey invited some women over for a night of pampering and I've never done this before, but I figured I should stock up on snacks. That's what you do when you have company, right?"

"You've never had friends over?" he asks, his tone one of disbelief.

"I . . . have. But never a big gathering. Well, not unless you count the study group, but they always brought their own snacks." I shrug. I have *tried* to have friends over. I once invited a girl from school over to watch a movie. She didn't talk the whole time, except to say thank you as she walked out while the credits were rolling. After that, she never talked to me again. I didn't try again after that, so I'm a bit wary about tonight. My first girl party.

"Okay," he says, grabbing several bags of chips from the shelves. "Let's get you ready for girls' night."

By the time we're checked out and loading the bags into my car, I've almost forgotten about roll-agedon. Until Lauren runs up and tosses a package of toilet paper into my open trunk before running away and getting into Miley's waiting car.

"Seriously?" Bradley calls after her, "Thanks, I knew we forgot something."

At that, Lauren's laughter stops, and Miley shoots him an evil glare and drives away.

"Thanks for that."

He shakes his head. "Those two were always trouble." He places the last bag into my trunk and pushes it closed. "I hope you have fun tonight," he says, stepping back and grabbing the bag of groceries he'd been there to buy.

"Thanks, I think I will."

"See you soon."

He turns to walk away when I realize I never thanked him for the flowers. "Hey, Bradley?" He stops and faces me. "Thanks for the flowers. They were beautiful."

"My pleasure," he says, walking away backwards until a car honks at him.

I watch him for a second, trying to wrap my mind around everything. In just a few days, Bradley's gone from an enemy to a . . . friend?

I pull out of the parking space and see Bradley still sitting in his truck. He waves to me, and pulls out, heading in the opposite direction. Hmm, was he waiting for me?

⸙ ⸙ ⸙ ⸙ ⸙

The girls are all here, conditioner in their hair, clay on their faces, eating snacks and laughing. No one is one-upping anyone, and everyone seems to be so genuine—not a catty one in the bunch. So far, at least. It's a nice surprise. It's been my experience that when you get a bunch of women together, they usually spend their time talking about people. Other than Lacey, and now Ashlan, I haven't had much luck in the friend department. Maybe my luck's changing. Finally.

"Stop wiggling your nose like that," Lacey says to me. "You're going to ruin your mask."

"It itches," I complain.

Karlee laughs. "It really does. I think they're dry enough. Can we wash them off now?"

"Fine," Lacey says, leading the way down the hallway to the bathroom. "I put a stack of towels on the counter. Feel free to wash it off."

One by one, the women wash their faces, careful to avoid getting their hair in the mix. Once my face is clean, I scratch my nose and sigh in relief.

"Time to wash out the conditioner," Anne says. "Care if I use your kitchen sink for that?"

I shake my head no.

Karlee is the first up. She leans over the sink, and Anne uses the detachable sprayer to rinse the goo from her hair.

"I heard someone knocked over a whole tower of toilet paper at the grocery store today," Briella says. "That would be so embarrassing."

I feel my cheeks turning red. I'd hoped my disaster wouldn't be gossip worthy, but here we are.

"It happens," Ashlan says. "Once, I picked up an orange that was apparently the glue holding the whole pyramid together. They went rolling all over the produce section." The girls laugh and Anne shares about a video she'd seen on TikTok where someone toppled over a display of feminine hygiene products.

"I'll be right back," I say, stepping into the hallway and down to the linen closet. I grab the package Lauren had tossed in my car and headed back to the kitchen. If these girls were my friends, they'd be embarrassed *with* me, not make fun of me, right? Guess we'll find out.

"It was me," I say, stepping back into the room with the toilet paper held high. "I knocked over the TP mountain. It was the wipe-out heard throughout Piney Brook."

Everyone gasps and giggles. "Oh my gosh, were you embarrassed?" Lacey asks, popping a chip into her mouth.

I nod. "I'm pretty sure if I could've disappeared, I would've."

"What did you do?" Karlee asks, her eyes as big as saucers.

"Well, I stood there in shock. Then Bradley came to my rescue." I feel heat creep up to my cheeks.

Lacey whoops and claps her hands together. "I knew he was your knight in shining armor!"

"More like her knight in denim and steel-toed boots," Anne says, smiling. "That man must be a saint to work with Hudson every day." She rolls her eyes, but I don't miss the blush that stains her cheeks, either.

"He's something," I say. What exactly? I'm not sure just yet.

Chapter Twelve

Bradley

THE SMELL OF CHARCOAL embers fills the air. Nothing like grilling a steak for dinner on a Saturday night. Especially when I've been working on a special project all afternoon. Once the steak is a perfect medium, I remove it from the grill and let it rest on the cutting board while I chop veggies for a salad. The key to a great steak is letting it rest. At least, that's what Dad always says. Once it's rested for a few minutes, I slice the steak into thin strips, add it to the top of the salad, and drizzle on the dressing. It's such a pleasant night, I decide to eat outside. Once I'm settled into the Adirondack chair on my back porch, I spear a piece of steak with my fork, and pop it into my mouth.

What a day. Seeing Aurora at the grocery store was a fun distraction. I laugh out loud when I remember how she'd looked with toilet paper packages falling all around her. Of course, I didn't laugh at the time. That would've been rude. Besides, she felt mortified, which became especially clear when she allowed me to hold her hand while we shopped together.

I rub my thumb across my fingers where they'd been touching her face earlier today. The feel of her skin on my hands is seared into my memory. I came so close to leaning in and kissing her lips, but I need her to trust me first.

I shake my head and take another bite of salad. I wonder how girls' night is going. Hopefully, she's having the time of her life. She works too hard. From what I can tell, she's at the Coffee Loft from sunup until after sundown most days. No one can go like that forever without getting burnt out.

It's hard for me to believe someone as wonderful as Aurora hasn't ever had a girls' night party before. She's been holding herself back. To think that Lauren and Miley still think it's okay to bully her is insane to me. Don't bullies usually grow up and stop treating people poorly to make themselves feel better?

I turn on some music—"Today's country hits"—and sit back in the chair to finish my food. No sense getting bothered over those women. Besides, I have a project to finish. Which reminds me—I need to call Mom.

I slip my phone out of my pocket and dial her number.

"Hi, son." My dad's voice carries across the line. "Your mom's in the shower. Everything okay?"

"Hi, Dad. How are you?" I miss my dad, but the last few times we talked it didn't end well. I know he means well, but he doesn't like to take no for an answer. Or admit he might be wrong.

"Good. Busy. You know how it is this time of year." Dad owns a retail store near the lake selling fishing and boating equipment.

"I do," I say. Dad's always wanted me to go into business with him, but I don't want to move to Colorado, which is where they headed after I graduated college.

"Well, I'll tell your mother you called," he says when the silence stretches on.

"Thanks, Dad."

Hanging up feels like a lead weight just dropped into my stomach. Ever since I moved back to Piney Brook, things have been more strained than ever.

Feeling antsy, I decide to sand down the wood I cut this afternoon. Once it's smooth, I can assemble and stain it all. According to the measurements Heath got for me, it should fit perfectly. If everything goes as planned, it will be a wonderful addition to the Coffee Loft. I just hope Aurora likes it.

When it gets dark, I turn everything off, unplug my tools, put them into the detached garage behind the duplex, and clean up my mess. A hot shower and a good night's sleep are in order. I hear my bed calling my name.

☕   ☕   ☕   ☕   ☕

Sunday morning, I slip on my running shoes and head out to the front door. There's a park with a trail just down the road, and I've been dying to run there. In high school, I joined the track team. Mostly to make my parents happy, but I discovered I really enjoyed it. Running lets me think things through, pound out my frustrations on the pavement, and it turns out . . . I love the runner's high.

I do my warm up—soldier kicks, leg swings, lunges—on the short walk to the entrance of the park. Once I find the trailhead, I take off

at an easy jog. I've not been down here before, and I want to take
it all in. I come to a fork in the path and jog in place while I decide
which way to go. The left leads to the lake according to a posted sign,
so that's the direction I head. The fall colors have taken over, and the
trees are a riot of orange and yellow. Leaves crunch under my feet as
I make my way down the dirt path. It's not long before I hear a dog
barking in the distance.

Keeping my steady pace, I breathe the cool morning air in through
my nose and out through my mouth. It's been a while since I made
time to run, and I can feel myself getting more centered the longer
I'm out here.

The sound of the dog barking is getting closer. Maybe I should get
a dog for a running partner. Or not. I'm gone long hours sometimes,
and that wouldn't be fair to a dog. I'm still debating the pros and
cons when I turn the corner and run smack dab into a loose dog,
trip over it, and land right in the muddy bank of the cold lake.

"Pax, get over here!" a woman shouts, running from the far side
of the lake. "I can't believe you!"

That voice sounds familiar. As the woman gets closer, I notice her
dark hair swinging wildly behind her. It can't be . . . "I didn't know
you had a dog," I say, standing and brushing as much of the muck
off myself as I can.

Aurora's mouth goes wide when she turns, leash in hand, and sees
me in all my mud-spattered glory. "I am so sorry," she says. "I'm dog
sitting for my parents this week. They just dropped him off an hour
ago, and I thought we'd start out with a nice walk. I can't believe he
got away like that!"

Pax is happily sniffing the grass along the sidewalk as though he
didn't just send me tumbling into my own mud bath. "It's okay," I

say, holding up my muddy hands. "I've been meaning to book a spa day. Besides, I'm washable."

"If you give me your clothes, I'll get them washed for you." She's struggling with the leash again as Pax, an Australian Shepherd mix from the looks of him, has found something interesting in the bushes and is dragging her along behind him. "Pax, stop!"

I squish my way back to dry land, wipe my shoes on the grass as best I can, and jog over to the chronic sniffender. I nearly snort at my own joke, but I doubt she'd appreciate the humor right now. "Here," I say, taking the leash. "I'll help you get him back to your car, but I think I'll have to wash my own clothes. No one wants to see me walk home naked and muddy."

Her lips open to a perfect little O. "You're probably right," she stutters, as her cheeks turn a brilliant shade of red. "Thanks for rescuing me. Again."

"Gladly. Where's your car?" I tug the leash, and Pax comes out of the bushes, a big stick in his mouth. "Come on, boy. You've caused enough trouble for one morning."

"This is why my parents hired a trainer. Though, from the looks of it, Pax could use a little more instruction time."

I laugh. "You're probably right. You said you're dog-sitting?"

Aurora falls in step beside me and I listen as she shares more about her parents, who are on a cruise for their anniversary.

"Here we are," she says, hitting the button on her key fob and opening the back door to her sedan. "Up, Pax." The dog jumps into the back seat where Aurora's covered the fabric with what appear to be old blankets. "How can I make this up to you?" she asks, waving her hand over my muddy clothes. "That looks so uncomfortable."

I look down and cringe. I'll probably need to hose off before heading inside. "No need to make it up. Things happen. It's not the first time I've fallen on a run."

She shakes her head, ready to argue with me.

"But if you want to join me for brunch, I won't say no." I sway back and forth on my stiffening sneakers while I wait for her to answer.

"I can't today," she says. "I'm afraid to leave this dog alone for too long. She's a disaster on four legs."

"Okay, no problem." I refuse to be that guy that can't take no for an answer. "See you around." I watch as she clips the dog into some seatbelt contraption and climbs inside her car. She smiles and gives me a little wave as she pulls out of the parking lot.

Nothing to do but clean up and finish that mug wall.

I just hope that it's one surprise that finally goes right.

Maybe it'll give her a reason to smile—and a reason to think of me.

Chapter Thirteen

Aurora

IT'S BEEN SEVERAL DAYS since I ran into Bradley at the park. Thankfully, my parents are back and picked up Pax this morning before I left for my shift at the Coffee Loft. I still can't believe he tripped Bradley and caused such a mess. I was so embarrassed and distracted by Pax's pulling that I didn't even think when I offered to take his clothes to wash them.

Thank goodness he seems to have a sense of humor, otherwise that could have gone so much worse.

I'm surprised I haven't seen Bradley in the Coffee Loft. Even though he's waved when he walks by, he's stayed away like I asked. I'm not sure how I feel about that. On one hand, I'm grateful he's giving me the space I asked for. On the other . . . I miss him popping in.

Heath and his co-worker Hudson were in early this morning to section off the part of the dining area that would be under construction. A huge barrier now separates the demolition zone from the rest of the shop. Thankfully, that means I can keep operating and won't lose much revenue.

"Well, then," Mrs. Sanders says, setting her book and purse at a nearby table. "It looks like you're in the home stretch." She leans against the counter while she takes in the makeshift wall the men put up.

I grin and busy myself making her a latte. "You're right. I'll be glad when this part is done. Lacey's next door, setting up the rooms and preparing the computer system today. Opening day is in a week!" I pass the latte over to her.

"Thanks, dear. I'll have a banana nut muffin, too, please."

I quickly plate the muffin for her and slide it across the counter. "Anything else?"

She shakes her head. "That's it for now."

I ring in her order, and take her payment just as the sound of hammers slamming into drywall starts.

"Oh dear . . . we may have to meet at the library today." Mrs. Sanders jumps at each crash of the hammer. "It's a bit too loud to think in here."

Her point is made when a loud buzzing starts from behind the barrier. "You're not wrong," I say. "I'm sorry. Can I get you a to-go cup?"

She smiles kindly. "That would be nice. I'm looking forward to seeing what it's like when it's all done." She's nearly shouting to be heard over the sound of things breaking.

I reach under the counter and grab a bag for her muffin and a cup to pour her latte in. "Me, too."

She puts her things into the containers and waves before grabbing her purse and book and heading out the door. She's already on the phone when she turns the corner. Presumably to reschedule the book club to a quieter location.

When another customer opens the door, hears the noise, and steps back out, I decide to close up for the day. No one wants to get their coffee here with all this noise. After going through the closing procedures, I take a piece of paper and write temporarily closed on it in big block letters. I tape it to the front door before letting myself out and locking the door behind me.

Looks like I'll need to close like Bradley suggested, after all.

Heath steps outside while I'm locking the door. "Too loud?" he asks when he sees me.

I nod. "It's been louder than I expected."

"We'll be done with this part and the framing by the end of the day. Tomorrow, Hudson and his friend Toby, will clean up the debris, and we'll get that door installed. Once the door's in, the loud part's nearly done. We'll add the door casing, which requires a nail gun, but that's quick. Then we will just need to touch up the paint, and we should be out of your hair."

"How long do you think that will take?"

"We'll finish the loud stuff by tomorrow afternoon at the latest. The door's in the lobby of the kids' place, so it won't take long once everything's set to put it up."

"Thanks, Heath. I guess I'll be closed tomorrow, too."

He frowns. "Sorry. Did they not tell you this would be loud?"

"No, Bradley warned me, but I didn't realize how loud it would actually be." Honestly, I didn't trust him. It felt like he'd wanted me to fail. Another time I misjudged him, apparently.

"Okay. Well, if we're able to get the noise part done before you open in the morning, I'll have Bradley let you know."

"Thanks."

He nods and stuffs his hands in his pocket. "No problem. Have a good day."

When I get to the car, I remember Ashlan's scheduled to come in this evening. I'll send her a text. My head's pounding too much from all the noise to talk on the phone. I just want to go home and crawl into bed with my sleep mask on.

I dig through my purse until I find my phone at the bottom. I swipe it and pull up the text conversation with Ashlan to type out my message.

> Coffee Loft is too loud. I closed for the rest of the day. Possibly tomorrow, too. Can you let Bexley know as well? I'll still pay you for your scheduled hours.

There, that should do it. I toss my phone back into my bag and start the car. For the first time in a long time, I'm looking forward to going home to the absolute quiet.

The next day I'm able to open just a few hours later than usual. True to his word, the glass door is in, and Hudson and Heath are finishing up the trim and paint. Ashlan's here, so I spend my morning in the office looking through applications and setting up interviews. At noon, I decide to step out and grab some lunch. I'm passing by the guys when I overhear part of their conversation.

"Any idea why Bradley isn't here today?" Heath asks.

Hudson laughs. "Man, you missed it."

"I did?" Heath asks, confused.

"Apparently, Aurora *really* doesn't like Bradley or something. She told him to stay out of the Coffee Loft. He looked like a kicked puppy when he came back to work last week."

Heath shakes his head. "No way. Aurora is too sweet for that."

"I absolutely am not," I say, coming up behind them. Shame threatens to swallow me whole. Of course he'd been upset. He'd done nothing wrong, and I blamed him for Miley's bad behavior. Again. I've got to stop doing that.

"Sorry," Heath says, blushing.

I laugh. "It's okay. Bradley and I go way back, and I thought he was a bully when we were kids. When there was a fuss here last week, I asked him to stay away. I'd rather not deal with drama."

"Really?" Heath asks. "That surprises me. I never pegged him to be the bullying type."

I put one hand on my hip and pin him with a serious look. "Well, there were some misunderstandings. Elementary school was brutal, and junior high wasn't any better. I'm fine with him now, but back then, not so much," I say before walking away to let Ashlan know I'm heading out. Bradley shared with me that he'd never intended to hurt me, and I believe him, but old hurts don't heal overnight. Even if I want them to.

"Ashlan, I'm stepping out to get some lunch. Want me to bring you something?" Ashlan has stepped into the role of my assistant manager seamlessly.

"No, thanks, I packed lunch today." She grins. "Take your time, though."

"Thanks. I think I'll head home for a while. If you need me, call me." I grab my purse from under the counter.

"Why don't you just take the rest of the day off? I'll be fine here. If I'm not, I'll call you." She shoos me away with her hands. "Go, relax. You'll be swamped with people coming in to see the final product once word gets out that the crew's finished with the noise."

I glance around the nearly empty space. She's right. Once people find out the Coffee Loft and Matti's Playhouse are connected and open for business, they'll want to see it. "If you're sure."

She grins. "Absolutely, boss."

"See you tomorrow, then."

I'm pulling up to my driveway when I spot Bradley's truck parked out front. What is he doing at my house? I park the car and get out.

"Uh, hey," Bradley says, stepping in front of a package on my porch. "I didn't think you'd be here."

I shake my head. "At my own house?" I move closer, trying to get a better look at what he's clearly trying to hide. "What's that?" I ask, pointing behind him.

"Oh, that," he says, stepping to the side. "That's nothing." He blushes. Bradley Jameson actually blushes.

"Nothing, huh?" I move closer, curious about this mysterious box of nothing.

"Well, it's not nothing," he stammers. "It's just not a big deal."

I start up the porch steps, when my foot gets caught on the second step and I go flying forward. Bradley jumps into motion, scooping me into his hard chest. A hum of electricity pulses through me. I should be embarrassed about nearly falling, but the only thing I can focus on is how good his arms feel around me.

His breathing stutters as his hold on me tightens. I can't draw my eyes from his full lips. I'm staring when he clears his throat, breaking the spell.

"Are you okay?" he asks, his voice barely over a whisper.

"I think so," I say, getting my balance and forcing myself out of his arms. *What was that?* Bradley Jameson, the person I blamed for all the mean things Miley and Lauren said and did, caused my brain to go haywire with a little catch? Who am I kidding? He's been making my brain go haywire since I saw him outside the Coffee Loft and tried to hide on the floor.

"Good," he says, shaking out his arms a little. "I was just dropping something by. It's nothing really, but I thought you might like it. Ashlan mentioned you were collecting unique coffee mugs, and I thought you might like some with your logo on them as well. If you don't like them, I can take them back. Well, probably not, but I can use them at my house or something."

He's cute when he's flustered. I mean, he's gorgeous all the time, but this side of him reminds me of when we were kids, before everything got so messed up.

He's so close I can smell his cologne. Woodsy, with a hint of something sweet. Perfect for him. "That looks like an awfully big box. How many did you order?"

He rubs his hand through his hair. "Uh, fifty? I figured you may want some to sell, or give away. I don't know. Fifty just seemed like a good number." He shrugs.

"Can I see them?" I step around him to the box on the porch. "Why don't you bring them inside?" I unlock the front door and swing it open. "Kitchen's straight back."

He bends down and lifts the box like it's a feather. Swoon! His biceps strain his t-shirt sleeves. Who knew arms could be hot? I'd certainly never cared about someone's arms before.

"Here you go," he says, setting the box on the kitchen table and opening it. Carefully, he takes a mug out of the packaging and holds it up for me to see.

The Coffee Loft logo is on top of a splash of watercolor. Pinks and teals swirl together, making the logo pop even more. "Wow, they're beautiful." I take it and turn it around in my hands. "I think the customers will love these. Thank you!" I lean in and give him a hug.

When I step back, he's beaming. His signature smirk is in place, and this afternoon it doesn't bother me.

"I know it's been a long time since we were friends, but I'd like to take you on a date. A real one, where I pick you up and take you somewhere nice. Would that be okay?"

I think back to sixth grade. How the girls called me Thumper when he complimented my hair. How they laughed and made fun of me when he sat by me, saying he must have felt sorry for the chubby girl. He'd been trying to be nice to me after all. My heart skips in my chest like it's playing double Dutch on the playground.

"You're thinking awfully hard, Aurora. It's okay to tell me no. I won't like it, but I'll understand." Bradley steps back, giving me room to breathe air that doesn't smell like him and clear my head.

"I'd like that."

Did I just agree to an actual date with Bradley?

I think I did.

Chapter Fourteen

Bradley

"I'd like that." Aurora's soft reply feels like an answer to a prayer.

I can't contain my smile. "When are you free?"

She laughs. "I'm off the rest of the day, and then I don't know. We've been looking to hire a few more people, but . . ."

I nod. "Tonight's perfect. Can I plan to pick you up at six?" I'm already mentally scanning my closet to make sure the one pair of slacks I own is clean. If not, I'll go out and buy another pair.

"Six is good. What should I wear?" I can see she's remembering our first date disaster.

"Whatever you'll feel most comfortable in. I'd like to take you to Surfside, if that's okay." She nods. "Great, I'll be back to pick you up in . . ." I glance at my watch. "Four hours."

She giggles, and I tuck the sound away in my heart. "See you then."

I lean in for a side hug at the same time she goes in for a hug and I end up smacking my head against hers. "Oh my gosh, I am so sorry."

She laughs. "That wasn't awkward at all."

Thankfully, the tension's broken and we are both laughing it out. "I'll be back," I say, holding out my hand.

She takes it and shakes. "It's a deal." Her laughter follows me all the way out her front door.

I'm so excited. The anticipation is greater than it had been when I'd asked her out the first time.

Once I'm back at the office, I dial my mom.

"Bradley, how did she like the mugs?" Mom's friend helped me with the custom order. She runs a printing shop and did the rush order as a favor.

"She loved them. Thank you for your help."

"I'm so glad," Mom says. "So, does that mean you're back on speaking terms?"

I take a breath to calm the butterflies that are trying to beat their way from my heart through my throat. "We are. In fact, she agreed to go on a date with me. Tonight." I pull the phone from my ear as Mom's shriek echoes through the office. "I'm glad you're excited," I say, my voice quivering with laughter.

"I'm just thrilled you actually like someone enough to pursue them. It's been a while."

After talking through my date plans and getting Mom's approval, she puts Dad on the phone.

"Mom tells me you've got a date with Aurora. Isn't that the girl you liked when you were a kid?" He sounds happy. Not at all like he's sounded the last few times we spoke.

"I do, and yeah."

"I'm glad it worked out. I was afraid when you moved back to Piney Brook, you'd get your heart broken again."

Wait, what? "What do you mean?"

"When we moved, I was pretty sure you'd never forgive us. Your main reason for wanting to stay in Piney Brook was Aurora, even if you didn't say exactly those words. Mom and I tried to figure out how to stay in Piney Brook, but money was tight, and I'd taken a new job in Lost Creek. We couldn't afford the commute back then. So, we had no choice but to move."

My mouth snaps shut. "I had no idea . . . You never said a word."

He clears his throat. "No father wants to admit he's a failure."

My eyes pinch closed in an attempt to stave off the tears. "Dad, you were never a failure. It ended up fine."

He sighs. "Yeah, but you built her up so much in your mind over the years that when you said you were planning to move back to Piney Brook, all I could think was you'd get there, and Aurora'd be married or something and you'd be upset you never got a chance to pursue her."

Finally, it clicks. "Is that why you pushed so hard for me to move to Colorado with you?"

Dad's quiet for a few minutes. "Well, it's not the only reason, but it's a big one. I wanted you to know you'd have a place here with us . . . you know, in case things weren't what you expected."

I shake my head. Of all the things I've thought over the years, none of these things were ever on my radar. "Thanks for sharing, Dad."

"You bet. Hope your date goes well. Call your Mom and let her know, okay?"

"Yes, sir. I love you, Dad."

"Love you, too," he says, then hangs up the phone.

I sit in the silence of my office and process what he'd just shared. I'd known he got a new job, but I hadn't realized we were under such financial strain. Though, thinking back, I can see the signs. How could I have been so selfish? I guess kids really are blind to their parents' struggles.

"Hey, boss, we're done. The trim's painted, and everything seems to be in order. Need anything else before we head out for the day?" Hudson stands in the doorway of the little room I've been using as a temporary office.

"Everything's cleaned up?"

He nods. "Everything but your junk," he says, motioning around the room. "Want us to help you toss it in a box?"

I shake my head. "Nah, I've got it. Go and enjoy your night."

He grins. "Thanks!"

"Oh, and Hudson," I call as he walks away. "Stay out of trouble."

"Got it, boss."

I pull into Aurora's driveway at 5:55, and grab the bouquet I picked up from Blooming Joy. Turns out Joy, the owner, is a sucker for a good romance story. She gave me a huge discount on today's order, and even told her assistant I'm becoming her best customer.

I make my way up her porch steps and notice the second step is loose—I'll have to get that fixed up for her. I'd hate to have her fall and get hurt. I lift my hand to knock on the door, but it swings open and is replaced by the most gorgeous face I've ever seen.

"Sorry," I say, jumping back and passing the flowers to her. "I meant to knock on the door."

Her eyes are wide in surprise. "I was just stepping out to wait for you on the porch." She brings the pink roses to her nose and inhales. "These are pretty, thank you."

"I hope they're okay. Joy, the florist, said roses were the way to go since I don't know what your favorite flowers are yet." I rock back on my heels, nerves making it nearly impossible to stand still.

"They're beautiful. I'll put them in water if we have a minute?"

"We do," I say, following her inside to the kitchen. "Why were you coming to the porch to wait?"

She shrugs. "I don't know. Habit I guess. I was engaged once, and he didn't like to have to come up to the door. So I'd wait outside and get in the car when he pulled up."

She was engaged? To a schmuck by the sounds of it. "You don't have to do that. I like coming to the door for you."

"Oh," she says, placing the roses in a tall crystal vase. "Okay."

Her cheeks are pink, just like the roses. "Sorry. I didn't mean to embarrass you."

"It's okay," she says, running her hands along her skirt and smoothing it out.

The cream and gold blouse she's wearing beautifully complements the deep burgundy of her skirt. She's beautiful in her jeans and Coffee Loft shirt, but dressed up, she's downright stunning.

"I seem to get flustered easily around you."

I smile. "I know the feeling. You look beautiful, by the way. Are you ready to go?"

She nods, and I follow her to the front door. "After you," I say once she's locked her front door. I take her hand in mine and help her down the steps and to the truck. Opening the car door, I step back and offer her a hand up. Once she's settled, I move to the driver's side and hop in.

"Is Surfside still okay, or should we get pizza again?" I'd love to treat her to something fancier than a slice of arcade pizza, but she's in control here, and I want her to know it.

"Surfside's perfect. I'm dressed for it this time." She lays her hands gently in her lap.

"All right," I say, backing out of her driveway. "Surfside it is."

Chapter Fifteen

Aurora

SURFSIDE IS AN UPSCALE restaurant . . . well, upscale for Northwest Arkansas, that is. The beautiful brick building is set back from the road on a small pond. There's a covered patio along the side with round tables for seating to allow for beautiful views of the lake and the surrounding mountains.

Bradley walks me to the front and pulls open the glass door. I step inside and immediately inhale the aroma of garlic and butter. My stomach grumbles.

"Can I help you?" the hostess asks.

"Table for two. The reservation's under Jameson." Bradley slides his hand over mine, and the zing I feel when we touch shoots straight to my heart.

The hostess grabs two menus and asks us to follow her through the elegant dining room. Deep blues and soft whites make up most of the decor. Some coral pieces add a touch of color to the dining room. The tables are covered in white linen, with vibrant sea-themed centerpieces, each a bit different from the next, as though they were handmade.

"Here we are," she says, pulling out my chair and placing a menu on the table. "Your server will be right with you."

Once we are both seated in the high-back chairs, I take a moment to soak it in. I'm on a date with a man who really likes me, at a restaurant I'd never come to alone. I consider pinching my leg, but decide against it. If this is a dream, don't wake me up!

"Good evening. I'll be your server tonight. My name's Ian. Can I offer you a taste of our house wine?" He holds out a bottle wrapped in a crisp white napkin.

Bradley waits to answer, giving me time to decide. "No, thanks," I reply. "I'll stick with water, please."

"The same," Bradley says. "But can we get an order of your shrimp cocktail as an appetizer?"

"Sure thing," Ian says, stepping away from the table to go put our order in and bring our drinks.

"I hope you like shrimp cocktail. It was one of my favorite things to order as a kid when we went to fancy restaurants." He grins like the boy I remember from elementary school. How could I have ever thought he was a bully?

"I don't know," I answer honestly. "I've never had it. My parents don't like seafood, so we rarely went anywhere with it on the menu."

"Oh. Well, here's to trying something new," Bradley says, reaching over and lacing his fingers through mine on the table-top. "Do you know what you'd like to eat?"

We discuss our options; him deciding on the surf and turf, and me the grilled salmon. Conversation flows, only stopping when Ian comes by with our food or refills of water.

"That was delicious," I say, patting my stomach. "I don't know that I've ever had lemon herb orzo before. It was tasty."

Bradley grins and scoots his chair back from the table a bit. "And you liked the shrimp cocktail, too. Seems it was a good night for new things." He winks.

"It would seem so." I'm too busy staring into his dark chocolate eyes to notice someone step close to the table.

"Well, look who it is. Thumper and Bambi. I swear, you two are too much." Miley laughs loudly. "Aren't they adorable, Martin?"

Martin, Miley's husband, I assume, barely spares us a glance, clearly uncomfortable with his wife's volume.

"I'm surprised you two got a table. This restaurant usually attracts a . . . different crowd."

I feel my face turning beet red. She always knew just what to say to make me feel unwelcome.

"Darling don't be nasty. You're drawing a crowd. Besides, I met you while you were employed at a convenience store—I hardly think that qualifies you to cast judgment on others. Enjoy your evening." Martin grabs her firmly by the elbow and pulls her away from our table.

"What just happened?" Bradley asks, watching them walk away.

"I'd say Miley Becket just got put in her place." I'd feel sorry for her, but her bullying has affected my life for years and almost ruined this . . . whatever this is.

"I'd say you're right," Bradley says, chuckling. "Would you like to celebrate with some dessert?"

I check my watch. "I really shouldn't. My shift starts early tomorrow."

He nods and motions for Ian to bring the check. "Rain check on dessert, then?" His eyes meet mine, a deeper question unasked in their depths.

"I'd love that."

The ride home is mostly quiet, but I can't help but feel like we've embarked on a new journey. One where Miley's shenanigans are out of the picture for good.

"You were right," I tell Ashlan the next day when she comes in. "We've been busy all day with people wanting to see the new space and peek through to Matti's Playhouse next door."

She grins. "I told ya. Is Ember starting tonight?"

Ember is the new girl who is going to train to be our third key holder. At eighteen, I was hesitant to hire her, but once I interviewed her, I knew she'd be perfect. She's hoping to save money to go to college. She wants to be an EMT and help out with the PBFD. "She is. Are you still comfortable training her?"

Ashlan gives me an "are you kidding" look. "Yes."

I wipe the sweat off my forehead with the back of my arm. "Thank goodness. I'm beat! I called and asked if Bexley can come in tomorrow right after school. If tomorrow's as busy as today was, I'll need the extra help."

Ashlan grimaces. "I'd come in earlier, but I can't get a babysitter on such short notice."

I spin around and face her. "A *what*, now?"

She ducks her head. "A babysitter. Usually my mom watches Ezra for me, but she's got jury duty this week, and my neighbor is helping me out."

I nod my head slowly. "Ashlan, why did you never mention you have a child?"

"I'm young, and I'm not married. Most of the jobs I applied for turned me down the minute they found out I had a kid at home." She grabs a towel and wipes down the espresso machine.

"I'm sorry that happened to you. I wish I'd known." She stiffens, so I hurry to continue. "Because I'd have made sure your schedule accommodated having a kiddo at home."

"It's usually not a big deal. Mom works from home, and Ezra's four now. He's a good kid. Plays by himself or colors if she has a meeting and needs him to be quiet." She smiles and pulls out her phone. "Want to see a picture?"

"Of course I do," I say, moving in closer. An adorable little boy with brown curly hair and light green eyes grins at the camera. "He's cute. I bet he'd get along great with Matti. You should ask Lacey about a play date."

Ashlan shakes her head. "I don't know. Once people know about Ezra, they treat me differently. Like I have a scarlet letter on my chest or something."

I feel for her. I can't imagine being a young single parent. If my memory serves me right, Ashlan's only twenty-two. Not terribly young to have a four-year-old, but certainly younger than most women who start a family. "I'm positive Lacey wouldn't think any differently of you."

"Think differently of you for what?" Lacey says, stepping up to the counter.

"Nothing," I blurt.

Ashlan sighs and passes her phone to Lacey.

"Cute kid! Is he your nephew?" She passes the phone back.

"No, he's my son." Ashlan tucks the phone back in her pocket, avoiding Lacey's eyes.

"Oh, we should get the boys together. I know Matti would love a play date with a new friend." Lacey's already pulling out her phone to look at her calendar. "If you don't mind them playing next door, I'd love to have him join us for free play any night next week. Free of charge, of course."

Ashlan smiles. "I'd like that," she says. "Ezra could use a play buddy."

"It's settled, then," Lacey says, sliding her phone back in her pocket. "Just let me know when you want to bring him, and I'll bring Matti."

The chime of the front door opening pulls us out of our little bubble. "Hey, Heath," I say, stepping up to the register. "What can I get you?"

"Think you could hook me up with one of your coffees?" He blows into his hands. "It's awfully chilly out there tonight."

"Sure, what would you like?"

"Just a hot coffee with cream and sugar. Nothing fancy like Bradley likes." Heath chuckles. "He had Ashlan make him some iced cookie something or other the other day. I don't think Hudson's ever letting that one go."

Ashlan giggles. "You'd be surprised how many men order the flavored drinks."

Heath shakes his head. "Not me, I'm a plain old coffee guy. Now, Gabby—she likes the sweet stuff."

"Good to know. And Bradley likes the sweet stuff too, huh?" I ask, already thinking of a way to surprise him.

"Yep, almost as much as he likes s'mores, which is saying something. He keeps s'mores granola bars in his briefcase." He laughs. "That man's got a huge sweet tooth."

Lacey points to the street where Bradley's just parked and gotten out of his truck. "Seems s'mores and coffee aren't the only things he's sweet on, huh, Aurora?"

"What on earth?" I ask, moving from behind the counter when I see Bradley lift a big contraption out of his truck. The huge wooden . . . something . . . looks heavy.

"I'm gonna go help him with that," Heath says, before heading out the door and across the street.

"What is that?" I ask Lacey. "Were you expecting something for next door?"

She shakes her head. "No, I have no clue what it is."

Bradley and Heath step inside, setting the wooden contraption down. "What's this?" I ask, walking up for a better look.

Chapter Sixteen

Bradley

"It's a shelf for your mug wall." I grin and point to the empty expanse above the back counter. "I figured it could go right there. Customers would see it when they come up to order, and you can showcase all the unique mugs you find." It feels like my heart and lungs have paused, like some weird video game moment, waiting for her reaction.

Aurora's eyes snap to mine. "Where did you get this? It looks expensive, Bradley. I can't afford this."

Heath laughs. "That's a good one."

I clear my throat. The last thing I want to do is embarrass her. "Why don't you grab my tool box from the truck, Heath?"

"Sure thing." He grabs the keys from my outstretched hand. "Where'd he get it?" He shakes his head and laughs as he pushes through the door to the street.

"What's so funny?" Aurora asks, confused.

"It didn't come from a store," I say, tapping the top of the wooden structure. "I made it."

She steps back and takes it in, looking at it as if it was the first time she's seen it.

I'm pretty proud of this project. The exquisite walnut-stained shelf will be perfect for the back wall. I designed it so that hexagonal spaces, which match the design on the flooring, join together to make up the shelves where the coffee mugs will sit.

"You made this? It's stunning." Aurora runs her hand over the smooth finish.

I can't contain my smile. "You like it?" I've been so nervous she might not like it. Especially because she didn't have any input into the design.

She nods. "Of course I do, but I'm serious. I can't afford this."

"Sure you can," I say, lifting it and moving it closer to the counter. "It's a gift."

Lacey claps her hands together slowly, gaining speed. "Well done, Bradley. Well done."

Ashlan giggles. "That's a grand gesture if I've ever seen one."

I take a little bow, grinning at them. "Thank you, but it only counts if Aurora likes it."

Lacey nods her head up and down like a bobblehead on a dashboard on a bumpy road. "She likes it. Tell the man you like it."

Aurora waves her hand at them. "Knock it off!" She turns and faces me, an expression on her beautiful face that I can't quite decipher. "Of course I like it. I'd be crazy not to. I just can't accept it."

"What?" Ashlan says, stepping in front of Aurora. "Yes, you can. The man went out of his way to hand-make this for you and your business. It would be rude not to accept it."

I stand there, watching the two glare daggers at each other.

Finally, Aurora breaks eye contact. "You're right. I just . . . No one has ever done something like this for me before. I don't know how to accept big gifts. I'm sorry." She looks down at her feet, the apples of her cheeks turning a sweet shade of pink.

"You deserve so much more than a shelf, Aurora," I say, just loud enough for her to hear. "I just hope you'll let me be the man to show you." Stepping back, I grab one end of the shelf and gesture towards the backroom of the Coffee Loft. "Can I move this to the back until closing? When everyone's cleared out of here, I'll get it hung for you."

"Oh," Ashlan says. "She was just leaving for the day, but I'll only be around until a little after nine. I can't stay long after closing, though." Ashlan wrings her hands. "Sorry."

"I'll come back and supervise," Aurora says. "I just need to grab something to eat first."

I turn to Aurora and smile. This night keeps getting better. "Is that right? Care to take me up on that rain check for dessert? Though, since you haven't eaten, I'd love to buy you dinner, too."

"Sure, that sounds good. Though, if you're too tired, you can always hang the shelf another day."

Heath comes back in the door holding the tool box. "Where are we putting it?"

"In the back for now. Care to meet me back here at nine to hang it up?" I ask. "I'll pay you for your time."

"Sure thing, boss, but you don't need to pay me. Happy to help out. It wasn't long ago I was trying to win over the woman of my dreams."

My heart pounds fast in my chest . . . He's right. I am trying to win over the woman of my dreams.

Heath and I move the shelf and tool box into the back, making sure not to knock any of the stacked boxes over.

"Sorry," Aurora says, shifting things out of the way. "We just got an order in and I haven't gotten it put away yet."

"No worries," Heath says, sliding the shelf close to the stack. "We're used to having things everywhere." He grins and follows us back through the swinging door to the front where there's now a line of customers waiting for their evening caffeine fix.

"Here's your coffee," Ashlan says, handing Heath his to-go cup. "On the house."

"Thanks. I'll be back later." He takes his drink and nods toward me. "First, I've got to take my girl to dinner."

"Have fun. Thanks for your help." I watch as Heath slips through the door. "Ready to go?" I ask. "I hear Beats and Eats has decent fried chicken and good pie."

"Let me grab my purse." She turns and disappears through the swinging door that leads to the back and the small office space I spotted a few minutes ago.

She comes back through the door, her purse on her shoulder. "Thanks, Ashlan. Let me know if you or Ember need anything. Her new-hire paperwork is filled out already, so tonight, just show her the ropes. I'll be back by nine."

"See ya later," Ashlan says in between helping customers.

I push open the door, allowing Aurora to step out before me. "You look beat. Are you sure you're up for dinner and staying to watch me put up the shelf? I'm sure we can get it done before Ashlan needs to leave."

She shakes her head. "I can't take the risk you'd run late. She has a son to get home to."

"She does?" I ask. I've never heard her speak about a son, though to be fair, I haven't spent a lot of time in the Coffee Loft getting to know the employees, either. Especially once Aurora asked me to stay away.

"I just found out today." She looks at me with sad and tired eyes. "I wish she had told me sooner."

I wrap my arm around her shoulder. "That's my girl, always worried about everyone else. Who worries about you?"

She stops in her tracks. "Am I?" she asks.

"Are you what?"

"Your girl."

Oh, shoot. It's way too fast. We've only gone on one date—I refuse to count the bad one. "Well, I hope we get there. I'd like for you to be my girlfriend. It's too soon, I know, and we're just getting on good footing. I've got to be honest, though—I always considered you my girl. Even in sixth grade."

She nods her head and starts walking again. "Okay."

I take her hand in mine, and we walk together in silence until we nearly reach the truck. "I tried standing up to them, you know. Lauren and Miley? I told them to leave you alone, but they obviously didn't listen. My mom said they were just jealous because I liked you and no one liked them." I smirk at that memory.

"You did? I had no idea."

I shrug. "We were kids. Just figuring out what attraction was, and all that entailed. That time was hard for us all in different ways, I think."

She leans into my side, and I put my arm back on her shoulders. "I guess maybe you're right."

I help her into the cab and drive the few blocks to Beats and Eats. Normally, I'd suggest walking, but the weather has definitely gotten colder today. The ride passes in comfortable quiet. "I think we may be in for an early snowstorm. What do you think?" I ask as I park the truck.

She steps down on to the parking lot and tips her head back to look at the sky. "I think you may be right."

After we're seated and place our orders, deciding to forgo food and skip straight to dessert—s'mores cheesecake for me and cherry pie for her—I can't help but ask the question that's been rattling in my head since we left the Coffee Loft. "What do you want, Aurora? I think I made it clear what I would like, but you haven't shared much about how you're feeling. Do you think we might get to the boyfriend and girlfriend phase one day?"

She leans back in the booth and studies me carefully. "I don't know . . ."

She pauses, and my heart sinks. I'll be happy just being her friend, but my heart will need some time to get on board because it's clearly in her hands already.

"I never expected this," she says. "But yeah, I think we could."

Elated. That's the only word to describe how I feel. "I'm glad. You know, once I got my license and a job, I started coming to Piney Brook every now and again, hoping to bump into you, but we never seemed to cross paths."

She blushes and averts her eyes. "I avoided you," she says. "I couldn't risk Miley seeing us talking and add fuel to her fire. She really was awful. I couldn't wait to graduate and go away to college. When I came back and she was gone, I felt like I could finally breathe."

I reach across the table and put my hand on hers. "I'm sorry she was so awful."

She shrugs. "I'm trying to let it go. Let's talk about something else, shall we?"

We share dessert, each taking a bite from the other's plate, and talk until it's nearly nine. "I can't believe they didn't kick us out," I say when I realize how much time we'd spent in their booth eating desserts and enjoying each other's company. "I left a huge tip."

She laughs. "I'm sure Patty will appreciate that."

"Ready to hang up your new mug wall?" I ask, opening her door and helping her up.

"Yep." She tries to stifle her yawn, but can't. "Then I'm going home and dropping into my bed."

I close her door and quickly get in the driver's seat. "We'll be quick."

Heath's already there when I pull the truck into the side lot. "Thanks for meeting me again."

Heath smiles and rubs his hands together. "No problem. I know you'd do the same for me."

True to my word, Heath and I have the mug wall hung, and all the mess cleaned up in under thirty minutes. "All set. What do you think?"

"That was fast," Aurora says, yawning again. "It looks great! Thank goodness you're done. I'm falling asleep sitting up."

"How about you let me drive you home?" I suggest. "I don't want you driving this tired."

She shakes her head and yawns again. "Can't. I have to be back here at five to open."

"Okay," I say, thinking quickly. "What if I drive you home and sleep on the couch? I'll bring you back first thing in the morning and then head home to get ready for work. I'm usually an early riser, anyway."

She stares at me, the "no" forming on her lips.

I raise both hands in the air. "No funny business. Seriously, I just want you to be safe."

"Fine," she says, yawning again. "But my couch isn't that comfortable. You can take the guest room."

I let out a sigh of relief. She's bone tired, and I'd hate for her to fall asleep at the wheel and crash. "Perfect."

Chapter Seventeen

Aurora

As BRADLEY PACKS UP to drive me home—and stay over, apparently—I can't stop staring at the mug wall . . . of course, it doesn't hurt that I got to watch Bradley's arms flex every time he shifted to put it in place.

No one has ever done anything this grand for me before. Sure, my parents bought me gifts, but they were generic for the most part. Things they thought I could use, or the popular thing that everyone wanted.

My dad may be a successful businessman now, but growing up, we struggled just like everyone else in this small town. Which is part of why, while he's helping me with my business, he's mostly a silent partner. Only stepping in to offer advice. He believes in hard work, making something of yourself, and pulling yourself up by your bootstraps.

"I'm ready when you are," Bradley says, entering the dining room from the back. "Trash has been taken out to the dumpster, and the back door is locked tight."

I push up from my seat at the bar, handing him a to-go cup.

"What's this?" he asks, taking a sip. I watch as his eyes go wide. "S'mores hot chocolate?"

I nod. "I thought you might like that."

He grins and takes another sip of the sweet concoction. "You need to add this to the menu, it's delicious!"

My smile turns into a yawn. "I'll think about it," I say, rubbing my eyes.

"Okay," Bradley says, grabbing his toolbox and keys. "Let's go."

Bradley takes my elbow with his free hand as we walk out the front door. "You certainly are a gentleman. When did that happen?" I tease.

He smiles. "My mom would be happy to hear you think so." He steps back and waits for me to lock up. "My dad's a great example of how to treat the woman in your life. He's always going out of his way to make Mom smile."

"That's nice," I say, thinking of my own parents. Mom and Dad certainly make each other laugh and smile. Mom's the only one I've seen be able to get Dad to totally relax.

Bradley leads me to his truck and helps me climb inside before closing the door and stashing his toolbox in the bed before going around to get in. "The weather's really looking questionable. Did you happen to check the forecast?"

I lay my head back on the headrest and sigh as the warmth from the truck's heater seeps through the coolness of my jeans. "Nope."

He chuckles. "Yeah, me neither."

I shrug. "It's probably just a cold front. I doubt we'll get snow this early in November."

He pulls out of the parking lot and onto the mainly deserted road. "You're probably right. I hope you have enough blankets for both of us. Just in case."

I snort. "I probably have more blankets than any sane person should own." Dad always said I have a bit of a blanket obsession, and it got worse when I learned how to crochet my own afghans.

I must fall asleep, because the next thing I know, Bradley's lifting me out of his truck and carrying me up the steps. "I can walk you know," I say, burying my face in his warm chest.

"I know," he murmurs. "But I enjoy holding you."

His soft words dance on my heart, cracking the thin layer of ice I'd kept in place to protect myself from him. "Oh." I'd argue that I'm too heavy, but he's not even winded as he takes the steps to the front door and sets me on my feet.

"Here we are." He keeps his hand on my lower back, steadying me. It's comforting. When Jayme used to do something like this, it felt so patronizing. Like he didn't believe I was capable of standing on my own two feet. I tuck that thought away to examine later.

"Thank you." I unlock the door and step inside. Seeing the little old house with fresh eyes. The living room, painted the greige color landlords seem to like these days, is small, but clean. The plush couch, a splurge, taking up most of the open space. I'm relieved when I don't see piles of dirty clothes or empty coffee cups sitting out anywhere.

"Relax," Bradley says, obviously aware of my discomfort. "Your house is perfect. Just like you."

I flick my wrist in the direction of the couch. "This is the living room, the kitchen is behind that wall, and the bathroom is the first door on the right." I motion for him to follow me down the hall. "This is the guest room," I say, opening the door and stepping back. It's not much. A double bed in the center, with an antique table as a nightstand set between the bed and the wall. A small dresser with a lamp, and a picture of my parents on their cruise on top.

"It's great. Thank you." Bradley steps inside and sits on the bed. "Comfy, too."

Unsure what to do now, I rub my hands up and down my arms. "I'm going to bed. I'll be right next door." I point to my own bedroom door. "If you need anything, help yourself."

He nods. "I'll be fine. Get some sleep."

I yawn, letting my eyes close for a moment. "I'll need to leave here by 4:45. Do you need me to wake you?"

He holds up his cell phone. "Nope, I've got it."

"There should be an extra toothbrush in the medicine cabinet. Towels are in the closet in the bathroom, and cups are in the cabinet by the fridge." I think I've covered it. Mostly, anyway.

"I'll be fine. Promise. Go sleep." He slips his shoes off and sets them neatly by the bed. For some reason, I'd expected him to kick them off and toss them across the room. His neatness makes me smile.

"Goodnight," I say, before turning on my heel and walking a few steps to my own room. Once inside, I shut and lock the door. I kick off my jeans and pull my dirty shirt over my head, leaving them in a heap on the floor. I wonder what Bradley would think about that.

I glance at my dresser across the room and decide to forgo pajamas. The door's locked, and Bradley promised no funny business, so I drop into bed and let sleep come.

🌣 🌣 🌣 🌣 🌣

The buzzing of my alarm cuts through the perfectly good dream I was having. I'd been in Bradley's arms as he carried me through the street with a coffee cup on my head. I could examine what that particular imagery meant, but I'd rather stay focused on the feel of his strong arms around me. I snuggle into the warm sheets and sigh.

"Aurora?" Bradley's voice carries through the closed door. "Are you awake?"

I grunt. "Yeah, I am. Do you need something?"

He chuckles. "Not a morning person?"

"Uh, no. Not really." Sighing, I throw back the covers, and immediately regret it. Goosebumps cover my arms and legs. "It's freezing in here!"

"Yeah, about that . . ." His tone doesn't sound promising.

"What?" I ask, hoping that it's something simple. I don't have much extra for a costly heating repair or anything like that.

"It looks like we're snowed in."

The reality of his statement hits me, and I start to panic. "Here? Now?"

"Yeah, here and now. I turned on the news. They are canceling schools today, and advising people to stay off the roads until they've been cleared."

Fabulous. How am I going to open the Coffee Loft? Wait, he said they've advised everyone to stay home. At least there won't be a line of people waiting for me. "I need to call Ashlan."

"I figured," he calls through the door. "I'll start a pot of coffee and see about making some breakfast."

Grabbing my phone, I punch in her number and wait.

"Hello?" Ashlan answers, her voice thick with sleep. "Is everything okay?"

"Shoot! I'm sorry. I should have waited for a later time to call. We're snowed in, and I can't get into the Coffee Loft." I hear her yawn and my guilt ramps up even more. "Don't worry about it. Call me when you're up and we can assess the situation then."

"Okay," she says. "Will do."

I hang up the phone and stare at myself in the mirror above my antique dresser. *Now what?*

A few minutes later, wearing the warmest sweats I could find and wrapped in my turquoise and tan afghan, I walk into the kitchen to see Bradley's behind poking out of the fridge.

"Good morning, beautiful," Bradley says, when he realizes I'm standing there gawking at him. "I found some eggs." He grins and holds up the carton. "Unfortunately, it looks like you don't have any bacon . . . or bread for that matter."

I slip onto the bar stool at the counter. "Nope. I've been at the Coffee Loft so much I'm hardly here for meals."

He nods. "I see that. Looks like you could use a day off. But today, hopefully they'll have the roads cleared soon and we can get you back to work. Or at least get to the grocery store."

He pulls out a skillet and sets it on the stove. "In the meantime, how would you like your eggs?"

The afghan slips off my shoulders, and I haul it back up. "How are you so cheerful so early?" I glance at the full coffee pot. "Especially before coffee?"

He steps to the cabinet and pulls down two mugs. "Cream and sugar? All I could find was powdered creamer." He raises an eyebrow in question.

"Like I said, I'm hardly ever here. The Coffee Loft has all the coffee and creamer I need. The stuff here is just in case of an emergency, or company." It really has been a long time since I had a full day at home. Hopefully with Ember nearly trained, and Ashlan taking over as my assistant manager, we can hire a few more part-timers and I can actually take some time for myself.

"No worries. I can drink just about anything." He pours two cups and doctors them up. "How's this?"

"Thank you," I say, taking a deep inhale of the rich aroma. "It's perfect."

He takes a drink from his steaming mug and grimaces before hiding it with a smile. "Delish."

I laugh, a deep belly laugh. "Liar."

He joins me. "You're right, but it beats no coffee."

I slide off the stool. "How about I make the eggs since you made the coffee?" I reach into the fridge and pull out the small container of butter.

He takes it from my hand and points back to the bar stool. "Nope. I've got it. When's the last time you let someone take care of you?"

"I, uh . . ." I honestly don't know.

"That's what I thought." He shakes his head. "Let me make breakfast. We can argue over who makes lunch later. Deal?"

Mentally running over what I have left in my pantry, I cringe. "Deal." Hopefully the roads are cleared by then, because unless he wants tuna and crackers. I'm not sure I've got anything to feed him.

Chapter Eighteen

Bradley

"So," I say, SETTING a plate of scrambled eggs in front of Aurora. "Are you a cat person or a dog person?"

She takes a bite of the eggs. "These are good. Fluffy." She takes another bite and swallows down some of her coffee. "I'm a dog person. You?"

I slap my hand on my chest in mock surprise. "That's it. I guess we aren't meant to be after all." She laughs and I revel in the sound. "I have a cat."

"What's its name?" she asks, pushing around the last of the egg on her plate.

"Bagel. He's a sweet little thing. He loves to cuddle and sleep." I finish my eggs and grab both our plates and take them to the sink.

"You cooked, I'll wash." Aurora stands and joins me at the sink. "Do you need to call someone to check on him?"

I glance at the clock. "I will when it's not so early. My neighbor can check in on him." Mr. O'Malley next door is retired and spends his days front porch sittin' as he calls it. He watches the kids walk to and from school, waves at the older women out for their daily stroll, and generally has his finger on the pulse of our little street.

"That's good," she says. "I don't hate cats by the way."

I hold back my smile . . . barely. She didn't like that joke. Why does that make my heart soar in my chest?

"Looks like we have a chance after all." I wink and grab the dish towel to dry the dishes and put them away. "What kind of movies do you like?"

"Are we playing twenty questions?" she asks, as she rinses the skillet and places it in the dish drainer.

I shrug. "May as well. What else do we have to do right now?"

She looks at me, her eyes straying to my lips before averting her gaze out the little window above her kitchen sink, a faint blush coloring her cheeks. "Not much."

"So . . ." I prompt.

"I prefer romcoms, but I also like action movies. Especially the superhero ones." She dries her hands on a towel and leans against the counter. "Your turn."

I purse my lips and look away like I'm thinking about it. "Well, superhero movies are good, but I really like sci-fi or fantasy movies."

"Like *Lord of the Rings*?" she asks.

"Yeah, or *Star Wars*." I lean against the opposite counter mirroring her posture. "What's your favorite thing to do in the snow?"

She shivers. "Stay inside. Did you happen to turn on the heater when you woke up?"

I shake my head. "No, I didn't know what you usually kept it set to, so I left it." She walks to the thermostat on the hallway wall just outside the kitchen and pushes some buttons. "There, that should help take the chill out of the air."

"What do you want to do now?" I ask, grateful for the heat I can feel coming through the vents. I almost stayed in bed this morning. I don't do so well with the cold, but I wasn't about to let her know that.

"We could watch a movie," she suggests. "Or play cards? I think I have a pack around here somewhere."

"Why don't you cue up a movie, and I'll make us both a fresh cup of coffee?" Her hair is in a messy bun on top of her head, and it wobbles when she nods.

"Sure. Thanks."

When she's out of sight, I let out a deep breath and bow my head. I'm not big on praying these days, but today, I could use some help. After sending up a prayer, I make the cups and join her in the living room.

She's curled up on the sofa, her feet under her, the beachy afghan covering her lap, and the remote in her hand. I can't think of a time she's ever been more beautiful. "Here we go," I say, handing her a mug. "What did you decide on?"

She grins and I know she's picked something sappy on purpose. "*My Girl*. It's one of my favorites."

Ouch. "Uh, okay." I settle into the couch beside her. "That's a sad one."

She shakes her head. "Yes, and no. Of course it's sad when her friend dies, but it's also a story of renewal and growing up. Vada goes through a lot, but she learns that she's got people around her who support her, too."

I ponder her description for a moment. "I hadn't thought of it that way. Here's hoping I don't cry." The last time I watched *My Girl* was with Mom and by the end we were both sobbing.

She presses play and settles back onto the couch. After a few minutes, she shifts, and her body leans closer to me. I take a chance, and drape my arm on the back of the sofa. I'm letting Aurora take the lead here. While I'd like to announce to the world I found my person, I get that she's been hurt in the past and needs some time.

When she leans into me and lays her head on my shoulder, I can't help but smile and squeeze her a little closer. By the end of the movie, my shirt is wet with her tears, and my arm is starting to go numb, but I wouldn't trade it for the world.

"See," she says, turning the T.V. off. "Isn't it great?"

I still don't see the appeal in watching a movie I know will make me cry, but I find myself agreeing. "Best movie I've seen in years."

Her smile lights up the room. "Now what?" She stands and stretches her back, groaning with the movement. "Should we check the status of the roads?"

I shake my head. "It won't make much difference until they get through your street, but I can go shovel the driveway and sidewalk. I need to call Mr. O'Malley and see if he'll check on Bagel."

She nods. "I'll join you. Let me go put on some snow pants."

Twenty minutes later, we are out in the cold, shovels in hand, working together to clear the driveway.

"I should invest in a snow blower," Aurora says. "I don't know if I could do this whole driveway myself." She stands and leans against the shovel handle. "This is hard."

I grin and wipe the sweat from my brow. "It is. But it feels good to be moving in the sunshine, don't you think?" Thwap. A snowball hits me square in the chest.

"Feels great," Aurora says giggling.

She launches another snowball at me, but this time I move and it misses. Leaning down, I scoop up some of the fluffy snow and pack it into a perfect sphere in my gloved hands. "You want to fight?" I tease, aiming for her pink and purple snow pants. I smirk, and let the snowball fly. It manages to hit her calf as she runs away.

"Truce," she says, holding up her hands in surrender and laughing. "I call a truce."

I dust the snow off my not-so-waterproof clothes. "I thought so." I reply, still grinning. "That was fun, though."

While I was cleaning myself off, she must have snuck around behind me, because all of a sudden, she stuffs a snowball down my shirt and the cold wet snow slides down my back, causing me to jump up and down in the driveway. "Cold. Cold. Ooohhh, you've done it now!"

Aurora takes off in a run, laughing like a kid who just discovered the joy of a snow day. I take off after her, not quite catching her. I love seeing her free and uninhibited.

After playfully chasing and dodging each other, I finally manage to catch her. Smiling, I spin her around to face me.

I stare at her lips, pink and full, wondering what it would be like to feel them on mine. When she sighs and moves a little closer, I decide to go for it. I take a step closer . . . my mind already buzzing with the thrill of finally touching her soft lips with mine . . . and slip on a patch of icy snow. Flailing my arms in a desperate attempt to stay upright, I manage to grab onto her coat, causing us both to tumble and land in the soft snow.

"Sorry," I say, rolling off of her and helping her sit up. "I slipped."

She smiles softly, a hint of laughter dancing in her eyes. "Does that mean you're not going to kiss me now?" she asks, her voice tinged with anticipation.

My heart leaps in my chest and does some acrobatics I've only seen performed at the Olympics before settling back down. "I'd like to kiss you," I say, leaving the ball in her court.

"Then what are you waiting for?" she whispers in invitation.

That's all I need. My heart races as I lean in and press my lips to hers. The world fades away, and nothing is left but the feel of her lips on mine and the sweet hum she makes. Relishing in the feel of her soft mouth finally against mine, I tilt my head and deepen the kiss. Her hands reach out and rest on my chest, and the touch feels like home.

I've dreamed of this kiss off and on since sixth grade, and nothing I imagined even comes close to her softness, and the electricity buzzing up my spine. I want to press my lips against hers every day of my life starting today. I wrap my arms around her and pull her close. I never want to let her go.

When she pulls away, we are both breathing heavily, and grinning from ear to ear. I push to my feet and help her stand back up, just as the snowplow comes barreling down the street, a wave of snow piling up against the curb. "Looks like we can leave soon."

She glances behind me at the driveway. "If we get this cleared we can."

Right, the driveway. We'd barely made a dent before we got side-tracked playing in the snow. "I'll keep shoveling while you go inside and change. Then we can head into town and see what's open."

"Thanks," she says, leaning in and placing a chaste kiss on my cheek. "This was fun." The brightness in her eyes and her rosy cheeks speak the truth of her words.

"It was." More fun than I've had in years, and it's all thanks to the woman whose pink and purple pants are making swishing noises as she walks toward the house.

Chapter Nineteen

Aurora

I STEP THROUGH THE front door and take off my snow boots. My fingers drift to my lips where Bradley's had been just a few minutes ago. I can still feel the tingle from his kiss, or maybe it's the snow. I shake my head. No, it was definitely that kiss. I've never been kissed like *that* before.

Even when Jayme and I were engaged, his kisses felt . . . friendly. Safe. Comfortable. They definitely didn't leave me breathless. I'm glad we didn't get married. If that's what kisses are supposed to feel like, Jayme and I were way off base.

I peek out the living room window and spot Bradley shoveling snow from the driveway. His jacket is wrapped around his waist, leaving his long-sleeved t-shirt stretched taut across his back. I shiver as I recall his strong arms carrying me up the stairs last night.

Is this what true chemistry is? This feeling? Am I falling for Bradley Jameson?

Butterflies dance in my stomach. I am. I'm falling for the choco-late-eyed charmer.

He turns and spots me standing in the window. Grinning, he gives me a little wave and blows me a kiss before getting back to work.

Swoon.

I think I've already fallen.

The streets are cleared, but most people are staying home, from the looks of it. Kids are taking advantage of the day off from school and are outside tossing snowballs, building forts, and lying in the yard making snow angels.

"Do you mind if we stop by my house, before I drop you off?" Bradley asks. "My clothes are a little wet."

I glance at his jeans which are wet nearly to the knees. "A little?" I ask.

"Okay, more than a little. My feet are freezing, and some crazy lady stuffed snow down my shirt." He laughs. "I was trying to be tough."

I shake my head. "No need. You're tough enough without getting hypothermia. Of course we can stop by your place. Besides, I think I'd like to meet Bagel. See if he can convert me."

He grins. "You're going to love him." Bradley flips on his blinker and takes the next right. "I'm just down here."

When he pulls into the snowy driveway of a little duplex, I'm surprised. It must show on my face.

"I'm just renting while I try to decide if I want to buy a fixer-upper or build something new." He turns the truck off, and gets out. He wades through the snow carefully, and comes to open my door.

"Guess no one's done your driveway yet," I say, sliding out of the truck and into his waiting arms. "Maybe I should have brought my snowsuit."

He chuckles. "Maybe next time. Come on, I need out of these wet clothes, and you have a kitty to meet."

I don't know what I expected when he opens the front door and lets me inside. Not this, though. The warm honey color of his sofa accents the olive green of the walls. Taupe pillows are tossed haphazardly onto the cushions, and a large braided rug in warm earthy colors covers the tile floors. "Wow, this is stunning," I say, stepping further inside the living room.

"Thanks," he says, toeing off his wet shoes and socks. "My mom helped me decorate. Insisted, even."

I nod. "She did a great job. I love this!" A soft meow pulls my attention from the array of family photos on the walls. A little face pokes out from behind the couch, the brown and cream of his face making him look a bit like a toasted bagel with cream cheese. "This must be Bagel," I say, crouching down and holding out my hand.

The cat sniffs in my direction, and then beelines past me and slips between Bradley's wet legs. Okay then.

"Bagel, I'd like you to meet Aurora," Bradley says, picking the cat up and holding him close to his chest. "She's a friend." He places his mouth near the cat's ear. "Hopefully, she'll be my girlfriend soon," he says in a stage whisper.

"Hi, Bagel," I say. I know I'm blushing when I reach out and scratch under his chin. Bagel starts to purr, so Bradley hands him over.

"You two bond while I shower and change. I'll be back in a minute." He leans in and presses a soft kiss on my temple. "It's nice to see you so relaxed."

He turns and walks down the short hallway and steps through the door on the right. Carefully, I take Bagel over to the couch and sit down with him in my lap. His sweet purrs going a mile a minute sound like a little motor bike. He settles into my lap and starts pressing his paws into my leg as though he's kneading dough.

"Making biscuits, little guy?" I ask. I hear the shower turn on and do my best to think about anything else.

There's a knock at the door, and I glance down the hall wondering if I should get it. The knock sounds again. This time a bit more persistent. Maybe it's the neighbor Bradley mentioned. I get to the door just as the person on the other side knocks again.

I open the door, careful to keep my leg in the way in case Bagel tries to run out, and find myself staring into the deepest blue eyes I've ever seen. Red hair cascades around the mystery woman's shoulders in waves. I reach up and smooth back my pony tail. "Can I help you?" I ask.

"Who are you?" the woman asks, disdain dripping from her words. "Where's Brad?"

"I'm Aurora," I say, sticking out my hand in a friendly gesture. The woman scoffs and steps back.

"What are you doing at my boyfriend's house?" The woman flips her hair over her shoulder and props a hand on the hip she's jutted out.

"Uh, your what?" I ask, stammering on my words. I look the woman over again. Tall, thin, beautiful, completely dolled up and feminine looking in her leggings, long sweater and boots.

"My boyfriend." She rolls her eyes. "Don't tell me Bradley didn't tell you."

I shake my head. "No, I can't say that he did." I swallow hard, my heart dropping into my stomach.

"Well, maybe he didn't think you needed to know. What are you doing, cat sitting?" She taps a booted toe on the pavement.

I shake my head at a loss for words. "He was just giving me a ride since the weather was questionable."

She smiles, though it doesn't quite reach her eyes. "How nice. I'll just come in and wait for him, then." She pushes through the door, strides boldly to the couch and makes herself at home.

"Oh, okay," I say, fighting back the tears that want to fall. "I'll just walk from here. It's not too far." I grab my purse and push through the door before I feel the first tear slip down my cheek.

He's seeing someone?

I've gone and fallen in love with a cheater. Just my luck.

I've barely made it to the end of the street, wiping my cheeks as I walk, when I hear Bradley call my name. A fresh wave of tears begins to fall. Not today. He will not see me like this.

"Aurora, please. Stop!"

I risk a glance behind me. The red-haired woman is standing in his driveway, hands on her hips looking livid while he runs down the street in just a pair of sweatpants. Flip flops on his feet, and no coat . . . "Please, wait. I'll just keep chasing you, and my feet are freezing!"

I stop, wiping the offensive wetness from my face. "What do you want?" I ask when he's close enough to hear me.

"You," he says, panting and dancing from foot to foot. "I want you. Forever."

I shake my head. "I don't share, and I won't be someone's secret."

He laughs. "Secret? Who said anything about sharing? Woman, have you not been hearing me? I love you. There's no one else for me. I haven't been on a date in months. Not since the first month I was back in town when I met Julie." He points behind him. "We went out, once, as friends. I thought she was interested in Hudson." He shrugs. "I have no idea where she got the misguided idea that I'd want her in my home or as my girlfriend."

I glance back to where the redhead is stomping off to her car parked on the side of the street. "Why did she just show up today, then?" I ask, the events of the morning leaving me feeling confused.

"I have no idea. She said she wanted to check on me after the storm. She tried to kiss me, but I dodged her and let her know in no uncertain terms I was already taken." He points to his feet. "Can we please finish this conversation in the house? I can't feel my toes."

I hesitate a moment, and then nod my head. "Okay."

"Thank you," he says, taking my cold hand in his.

"I'm sorry," I whisper as we walk back to his house. "She said you were together, and I panicked."

"It's okay," he says, kissing the back of my hand. "I probably would have reacted similarly. In fact, if someone else tried to claim my future wife, I'd probably lose my mind."

My mouth drops open in shock. "What did you say?"

He gives me his signature smirk. "One day, I'm going to propose to you. You're it for me, Aurora. I think you always have been. No one else compares."

I shake my head. "You don't mean that. She's flawless. I'm just . . ." I pause, at a loss for the right words. "Frumpy. You'll get tired of me eventually."

Stepping closer, he presses a soft kiss on my lips. "Aurora, you're the most stunning woman I've ever known," he says. "I'll never tire of you. I love you."

"You mean it?" I ask, hope lighting like a spark to ignite my heart.

"Always," he says, his deep voice seeping into the parts of me that still questioned him.

I lay my head on his chest and breathe him in. This beautiful man loves me. He's mine, and I'm his.

Forever.

Chapter Twenty
Bradley

Six Months Later

"So," Heath says, stepping inside my office and leaning against the wall. "Are we still on for tonight?"

"Yep," I say, patting my pocket. "I'm ready." Heath has been helping me with an epic surprise for Aurora. After the snowstorm, we officially became a couple, and I went on the hunt for the perfect house to build a family in.

For the past few months, Heath's been helping me renovate the old farmhouse. To keep this secret, I had to tell Aurora I was working on a special project for my favorite client after-hours. She's been begging to meet this mystery client, and today, she finds out it's been her all along.

Mom's just cleaned up from putting the finishing touches on the paint. I figured since Aurora loved what she did in my apartment, I'd let Mom have free reign of the house. Though, if Aurora doesn't like something, I'll change it in a heartbeat. After all, this is where we will spend the rest of our lives together.

"See you at six," Heath says.

"Thanks," I say, pulling out my phone to message Lacey and make sure Aurora's ready.

> **Still on track?**
>
> > **I've got this. She'll be there. Don't you worry.**
>
> **Thanks. I owe you.**
>
> > **Ha! I know.**

I shake my head. Lacey is something else. Full of energy and love for those around her. Not for the first time, I'm glad she's on my side.

I push away from the desk and step into the small bathroom to change. I unzip the hanging bag and feel my throat start to tighten up. Never in a million years did I imagine I'd willingly put one of these things on.

I shuck off my dirty clothes, careful to put the ring box on the counter, and step into the suit I rented for this evening. I leave the top button undone, and the tie loose. I'll do those up at the last minute. I stuff my discarded jeans and polo shirt into the bottom of the bag and zip it back up. Taking everything to the truck, I toss it in the passenger side and climb up. It's go time.

Over the last six months, Aurora and I have spent all our free time together. We've gone on hikes, gone bowling, spent time with each other's families, and through it all, I've fallen more and more in love with her. Once she got used to the idea that she was precious to me, she opened her heart completely to me and let most of her insecurities go, so I've gotten to know even more of her than before, and I love all of it.

I pat the jacket pocket, relieved when I feel the box tucked inside. I make the turn off and head down the bumpy driveway to our new home. Well, if she says yes, that is.

Nerves are getting to me. I wipe my sweaty palms on the dress pants and pray I can keep it together. I've rehearsed this a thousand times in my mind. I want to get it just right.

Finally, I pull up to the driveway where several other cars are already parked and step out of the truck. Mom rushes down the steps to greet me.

"Let me help you," she says, buttoning the top button and fussing with the tie.

Dad steps to my side and pats my shoulder. "Never thought I'd see the day," he says, a smile tugging at his lips. "I'm proud of you, son."

"Thanks, Dad. And thanks for flying in and helping." Aurora is the light of my parents' eyes. Sometimes I swear they like her more than me. That's okay, though. I'm glad they love her as much as I do.

"Are you ready?" Mrs. Maxwell asks. She asked me to call her Tammy, but I just can't bring myself to do it.

"Yes, ma'am."

Mr. Maxwell nods and shakes my hand. "Take care of her."

I meet his eyes and nod. "I intend to, sir."

He pats my shoulder. "All right," he calls to the others. "Inside. She'll be here any minute."

We all make our way inside and I position myself just inside the foyer. When I hear Lacey's car pull up, I drop to one knee and hold out the ring box.

"Where are we?" I hear Aurora ask. "Lacey! You can't just walk into someone's house!" The door swings open, and Lacey rushes inside to take her place beside Knox and Matti. Aurora steps up to the open doorway and peeks inside.

When she finds me on one knee, she gasps and slaps both hands over her mouth.

"Well, come in, dear," her mom says.

Aurora carefully steps inside, never breaking eye contact with me.

"Aurora Laine Maxwell, I've spent more than half of my life wondering if you were the one that got away. When you blessed me with another chance to get to know you, my feelings grew deep and fast. I knew I needed to give you some time to catch up."

The crowd chuckles.

"When fate brought us together, I was determined to see if we had the spark that lights the fire of forever, and I believe we do." She nods her head. I reach for her hand, and she laces her fingers through mine. "Aurora, I would love nothing more than to spend the rest of my life falling more and more in love with you each day. Will you marry me?"

I hear sniffles, and I assume it's either her mom or mine.

Aurora glances around the room, taking in all the faces of the people who love her, before turning her face back to mine. "Yes," she says, nodding her head. "I'll marry you!"

I slip the half-carat platinum princess-cut diamond ring on her finger and kiss the top of her hand before standing and pulling her into my arms. "Thank you," I whisper into her hair. "You've made me the happiest man in the world."

She giggles.

"And your hair is way softer than my bunny's was."

She laughs and places a kiss on my lips. "You just think that because you love me. I love you too." She hugs me again, and when she steps back, she is bombarded with hugs from friends and family who are anxious to wish us both their congratulations.

"Come on into the kitchen and have some punch and finger foods," Mom says as the excitement dims to a manageable level. "Let's give the lovebirds a moment."

Everyone funnels into the open kitchen and dining area, and for the first time, I'm alone with my bride-to-be.

"Where are we?" she asks, looking around. "Is that your couch?"

I take her by the hands and walk her over to the sill of the bay window across from the sofa. I sit and she follows suit. "We're home," I say, holding my breath. "If you like it, that is. If not, I'll sell it and we'll find something else."

She looks around the living room. "It's *our* home? What do you mean?"

I take her hands in mine. "I bought it, and over the last few months, Heath and I have been remodeling it, then my mom came and decorated."

"Can I see it?" she asks.

"Of course." I take her by the hand and lead her through the house, saving the kitchen for last. The sprawling ranch house is large and laid out well with the bedrooms and bathrooms on one end, and the main living area on the other. We slip down the hallway where I show her the guest room first. "I figured your guest room furniture would fit nicely in here."

"It's a good size for a guest room," she agrees.

Moving on, I take her into the first bedroom. "This could be an office space, or a kid's room one day," I say opening the closet so she can see the space. I close it and lead her to another doorway. "This leads into the bathroom." The newly renovated bathroom boasts warm earth tones I know she loves. Her eyes are all lit up, so I know she's loving it. I lead her past the tub to the other doorway in the bathroom and open it up. "And this is the second bedroom," I say.

"Wow, these are huge!" She spins a circle. "I love it all so much!" She leans in and gives me a kiss.

"I'm glad." I take her hand, and we cross the hallway into the primary bedroom.

"Wow," she whispers, taking it all in. "Is that . . . Did you make that?" she asks, pointing out the handmade headboard.

"I did. Do you like it?"

She walks to the headboard and runs her hands along the carved design. "It's stunning."

I show her the primary bathroom and guide her back into the hallway. "What do you think?"

She hugs me and rests her head on my chest. "I love it. It's perfect. Just like you."

I hold her against me for a few minutes before I hear her mother calling for us.

"Looks like our tour is over," I whisper into her hair.

"But our life's just beginning," she says, just before placing a kiss on the corner of my mouth.

She's right. Our life is just beginning, and the best is yet to come.

Thank you for reading *You Mocha Me Crazy*! It would mean the world to me if you'd consider leaving a review.

Can't get enough of Tia Marlee? Check out *His to Have*, book 1 in the Apple Blossom Ranch Series, and keep reading for a sneak peak of chapter one!

I'd love to stay in touch. You can join my newsletter at tiamarlee .com/newsletter, and be the first to know about upcoming releases, sales, and more!

An Excerpt from His to Have

Apple Blossom Ranch
Series Book 1

Patty

Working the morning shift certainly has its perks. Except for the fact I'm not a morning person. I slide my non-skid shoes on and head for the kitchen to grab my steaming mug of coffee. I glance over at my unmade bed and shrug as I take a sip of the nectar of the morning. It can stay unmade. No one's going to be upset about it.

The small studio apartment above the garage of an elderly woman was heaven sent when I rolled into Piney Brook a few months ago. I fell in love with the small town's charm and decided to stop for a few days. At the time, I'd been thinking I'd go further west, but something about Piney Brook called to me. So, one morning, I stopped into the diner for breakfast and spread out the local paper on the table in front of me circling jobs and rentals that I might be able to get.

When Ms. Daisy saw what I was up to, she offered me a job on the spot. I swear she has a sixth sense about people in need. I took her up on her offer, especially because she didn't mind that I didn't have any experience. "We all start somewhere," she said. By the time I'd finished my first shift, she'd convinced her friend to lease me the studio space above her garage.

A far cry from the stuffy run-down trailer I'd lived in with Klive. I shiver and grab my keys. Getting away from Dixie Pass, Tennessee, and Klive, was the best decision I've ever made.

I step out of the apartment and close the door, locking it securely behind me. Taking the steps two at a time, I make it to the driveway in record time. I might not be late after all.

My light blue Honda Civic, the only possession I'd taken with me when I got married, and the only thing I'd left with, is waiting for me. I pat the hood as I walk by to open the door and slide inside. It's twenty years old, but the ole gal still runs perfectly. Okay, maybe not perfectly, I think as I start it and hear the whine of the belt I haven't had fixed yet. "Please, Gertie, just a while longer."

I pull out of the parking lot and head toward town. Of course I get stopped at both red lights between Mrs. Beck's house and Beats and Eats. By the time I park and make it inside to clock in, I'm five minutes late.

I stick my things in the back, and tie on my apron. Time to get busy.

Several hours later, we've made it through the breakfast rush, and most of the lunch rush. I've only got one table, and I'm grateful for the break.

"Order's up," Ricky calls from the kitchen.

I grab a tray and take the plates from the window, situating them so I won't drop them. "Thanks, Ricky," I say, sliding the tray onto one hand and balancing it with the other. I've been at Beats and Eats for a few months now, and while it's harder than I expected, it's also a lot more fun than I could have imagined. Every day is as different as it is the same.

After the way I lived before . . . let's just say it's a nice change of pace. Though it did take me a few weeks to stop jumping every time Ricky yelled through to the servers. Taking the tray of delicious smelling food, I tread carefully around the corner of the counter and into the dining room.

I stop at the table, balancing the tray on my arm. "A club sandwich, fries, and a side of ranch," I say, handing Gabby, my co-worker, her order. "And a BLT with a side of onion rings." I put Anne's plate in front of her. Making a mental note to call her for an appointment to get my hair done. I'm overdue for a spruce-up, and her salon is the best in town. And not just because it's the only one in town.

"Thanks, Patty," Anne says, dipping an onion ring in Gabby's ranch. "When are you going to let me jazz up your hair?"

I laugh. "I am due for a trim," I say. "Just a trim, though. I'm not ready to go crazy."

She grins and points her half-eaten onion ring in my direction. "One of these days, we are busting you out of your shell."

I hear the bell near the door jingle and glance that way. Ms. Daisy is smiling ear to ear and grabbing menus for the newcomers. "Don't look now," I whisper to the women who have slowly become my friends, "but there's a trio of guys that just walked in that I haven't seen before." I fan myself with my free hand. "I don't think they're from around here." I wink at them both. Gabby's only got eyes for her ex, Heath, but Anne's been talking about finding love. "I'd for sure remember *them*."

Anne chews her bite of food and looks over her shoulder to where I'd motioned. She spins back around, fanning her flushed face. "Oh my," she says, taking a sip of her pop.

"Told ya," I say, bumping my hip against the table before walking away to greet the men now comfortably seated in my station. If only I was as carefree and open to love as Anne. I sigh and clear my throat as I approach the table.

"Hi there, gentlemen. What can I get you to drink?" The three men seated at the table share the same features. Dark brown hair, blue-green eyes, and matching smiles that could blind oncoming traffic. So, brothers, I'm guessing. The one closest to me has little dimple marks on his smoothly shaven cheeks.

Swoon.

I listen as they rattle off their drink order. Sweet teas all around. I grin. "I'll get those right out. My name's Patty, if you need any-thing."

Dimples winks. "Thanks, sugar." He jerks and leans down to rub his shin. "What was that for?"

The guy sitting across from him smirks. "You can't go around calling people 'sugar.'" He shakes his head. "That's a lawsuit waiting to happen."

I chuckle and shake my head. "'Sugar' is fine with me." I wink. I feel the heat start to bloom in my cheeks. *What's wrong with me?*

"Be right back with your drinks," I squeak out. Turning on my heel, I rush to the drink station and start filling cups with ice. My hands are shaking, and I'm debating dunking my face right into the ice bin.

Who winks at a customer?

A very handsome, drool-worthy customer, but still.

I groan. After my divorce from Klive, you'd think I'd have permanent blinders on. I shudder at the thought.

"You gonna make those drinks or wait till the ice melts?" Ms. Daisy's voice startles me and I drop the cup I'm holding, scattering ice everywhere.

"I . . . I'm so sorry, I'll clean that up."

Ms. Daisy laughs. "Just finish making the drinks. I've got the mess." She grabs the broom and dustpan from in the corner and starts sweeping up the spill.

I remake the glass I spilled and add the tea before putting them on a tray and making my way back to the waiting table. "Here we are," I say, carefully placing the drinks on the table. "Sorry about that," I say, sneaking a peek at their left hands. No wedding rings.

"No problem, *sugar*." The man looks pointedly across the table, then turns back to me. "My name's Finn."

I blush. I can feel my cheeks burn with the increased blood flow. Drat having fair skin! "Hello, Finn, and who do you have joining you?" It seems silly to hold introductions, but I appreciate Finn's manners.

"These are two of my brothers, Caleb and Cooper."

I smile at each one in turn. "Nice to meet you. Have y'all decided on what you're having?"

"What would you suggest?" Finn asks. His eyes hold mine a beat longer than necessary.

"I like just about everything here, but you can't go wrong with Ms. Daisy's fried chicken." It's true. I've tried nearly everything on the menu here, and it's all delicious, but the fried chicken is next level.

"Great," Finn says, laying the menu on the table. "That's what I'll have."

His brothers chime in, both asking for the same.

"Perfect," I say, tucking my notepad into my apron. "That should be right out."

"Take your time," Caleb says, leaning back in the chair. "I'm in no hurry."

Cooper scoffs and says something I can't quite make out as I walk away. They sure are handsome, and did he say two *of* his brothers? How many men are running around in the world with those genes?

***

Get *His to Have* on Amazon today and fall in love with Patty and Finn.

A rancher, a waitress, and an unexpected bond...

Finn Miller has been working tirelessly since his uncle retired, leaving him in charge of Apple Blossom Ranch. However, there's a catch: Finn must get married by his thirtieth birthday, or the ranch will be sold, ending generations of his family's legacy. Determined not to lose everything, Finn is desperate to find a solution.

Patty Walsh moved to Piney Brook to escape an abusive ex-husband, seeking a fresh start in the small town. But starting over isn't as simple as she hoped. When Finn, a handsome regular at Beats and Eats, shares his predicament, Patty sees a chance to help him—and herself.

What begins as a practical arrangement might just blossom into true love. Can a business deal built on necessity transform into a heartfelt romance?

Welcome to the Coffee Loft

Welcome back to The Coffee Loft, where a new round of stories has been brewed especially for you.

Those of you stopping by to visit again, we've missed you. The feeling of home is the same that you loved before. If it's your first time, prepare to be swept off your feet. While our menu hasn't changed, we think you'll be pleased with the fall favorites we've added. Fans of pumpkin spiced lattes, peppermint mochas, and rich, chocolaty cocoas will not be disappointed.

This multi-author collection of stand-alone sweet romcoms is filled to the brim with the swoons you love and adore. From sweet kisses to grand gestures and matchmaking surprises, each mug and story will be filled with everything you crave.

So come on in and let us serve you with that happy ever after you've come to expect.

Find the entire fall collection on Amazon.

Did you miss the first season? Find them on Amazon.

Also By Tia Marlee

Piney Brook Wishes Series
His Christmas Wish
Sweet Summertime Wishes
Wishing for the Girl Next Door
A Soldier's Wish

The Coffee Loft Series
Bean Wishing for a Latte Love
You Mocha Me Crazy

Apple Blossom Ranch Series
His to Have
His to Hold
His to Love
His to Cherish
Hers to Treasure

About the Author

Tia Marlee enjoys delivering swoon worthy HEA's in her clean and wholesome romance novels. A small-town girl at heart, Tia's stories have that small-town, Hallmark charm with a dash of real life, and a laugh thrown in for good measure.

Tia is the author of the Piney Book Wishes series featuring unexpected love stories based in small-town Piney Brook, Arkansas. She is also proud to be part of the multi-author romcom series The Coffee Loft season one and two.

Tia resides in Texas with her husband and three teenaged children. When she's not writing or reading, you can find her standing barefoot in her front yard, loving on her 80-pound lap dog, or hauling kids from one activity to the next.

Printed in Great Britain
by Amazon

49560991R00101